HARRISON'S HEART

Heroes for Hire, Book 7

Dale Mayer

Books in This Series:

Levi's Legend: Heroes for Hire, Book 1
Stone's Surrender: Heroes for Hire, Book 2
Merk's Mistake: Heroes for Hire, Book 3
Rhodes's Reward: Heroes for Hire, Book 4
Flynn's Firecracker: Heroes for Hire, Book 5
Logan's Light: Heroes for Hire, Book 6
Harrison's Heart: Heroes for Hire, Book 7
Saul's Sweetheart: Heroes for Hire, Book 8
Dakota's Delight: Heroes for Hire, Book 9
Michael's Mercy: Heroes for Hire, Book 10
Jarrod's Jewel: Heroes for Hire, Book 11

Books in the SEALs of Honor Series:

Mason: SEALs of Honor, Book 1

Hawk: SEALs of Honor, Book 2

Dane: SEALs of Honor, Book 3

Swede: SEALs of Honor, Book 4

Shadow: SEALs of Honor, Book 5

Cooper: SEALs of Honor, Book 6

Markus: SEALs of Honor, Book 7

Evan: SEALs of Honor, Book 8

Mason's Wish: SEALs of Honor, Book 9

Chase: SEALs of Honor, Book 10

Brett: SEALs of Honor, Book 11

Devlin: SEALs of Honor, Book 12

Easton: SEALs of Honor, Book 13

SEALs of Honor, Books 1–3

SEALs of Honor, Books 4–6

SEALs of Honor, Books 7–10

HARRISON'S HEART: HEROES FOR HIRE, BOOK 7
Dale Mayer
Valley Publishing

Copyright © 2017

All rights reserved. Except for use in any review, the reproduction or utilization of this work in whole or in part by any electronic, mechanical or other means, now known or hereafter invented, including xerography, photocopying and recording, or in any information storage or retrieval system, is forbidden without the written permission of the publisher.

This is a work of fiction. Names, characters, places, brands, media, and incidents are either the product of the author's imagination or are used fictitiously. Any resemblance to actual events, locales, or persons, living or dead, is entirely coincidental.

ISBN-13: 978-1-773360-41-6
Print Edition

Back Cover

Welcome to *Harrison's Heart*, book 7 in *Heroes for Hire*, reconnecting readers with the unforgettable men from *SEALs of Honor* in a new series of action-packed, page turning romantic suspense that fans have come to expect from USA TODAY Bestselling author Dale Mayer.

When a call for help comes from Ice's father, Harrison steps up. A senator has been shot, his wife beaten and his kids are in the wind. It's up to Harrison to find the answers everyone is looking for.

Including finding the senator's ex-military and pissed at the world daughter. Only she doesn't want anything to do with him.

Zoe is on a mission. There's no room in her world for heroes – especially not Harrison. But he won't take no for an answer. Only Zoe has angered the wrong people, and they won't stop until they put an end to her meddling or better yet – to her.

With so much going on, Harrison struggles to pull the pieces together – before their world is completely blown apart – permanently.

Sign up to be notified of all Dale's releases here!

http://dalemayer.com/category/blog/

Your Free Book Awaits!

KILL OR BE KILLED

Part of an elite SEAL team, Mason takes on the dangerous jobs no one else wants to do – or can do. When he's on a mission, he's focused and dedicated. When he's not, he plays as hard as he fights.

Until he meets a woman he can't have but can't forget. Software developer, Tesla lost her brother in combat and has no intention of getting close to someone else in the military. Determined to save other US soldiers from a similar fate, she's created a program that could save lives. But other countries know about the program, and they won't stop until they get it – and get her.

Time is running out… For her… For him… For them…

DOWNLOAD a ***complimentary*** copy of MASON? Just tell me where to send it!

http://dalemayer.com/sealsmason/

Chapter 1

HARRISON HAMILTON SAT down at the dining table, his movements jerky, rough, and almost ending with his coffee washing the tabletop. At least only Levi was here. Harrison stared at his cup glumly. He was going nuts here. He raised his gaze and glared at Levi. "Get me the hell out of here. You must have a job somewhere for me."

Levi raised one eyebrow. "Walls closing in on you?"

"The compound of love is getting to me." He leaned forward. "You know what it's like to be the only single guy here?"

Levi barely held back a smirk. "That'll change. We got a few more guys coming in."

Harrison nodded. "That's nice. But they aren't here now. I tried to watch a movie last night, and people were cuddling on the couch. I went to the kitchen to get away from that, to work on a report, and found another couple cuddling." He rolled his eyes. "I went to the goddamn gym to work off some of that lovely extra energy, and what did I see? Another couple. I'm coupled out." He picked up his coffee and drank half of it all at once, then put it down and said, "Find me a job and get me the hell out of here." He groaned and stood to leave when he heard the crowd coming for breakfast. "Here we go again." He dropped to his chair in defeat.

Levi shook his head, a frown forming. "Don't take it so personally."

Harrison glared at him again. "It's not that it's personal. It's overwhelming."

Levi's face relaxed. "I can see that. I remember when …"

"Yeah, when it was just us guys." Harrison didn't bother to explain his acceptance of Ice as *one of the guys*, bringing the expanded original team count to seven. "Now it's me against, what? How many of you? … Six! Plus your partners. It's ridiculous."

Couples streamed in, looking for morning coffee and food. With bright cheerful chatter, several headed for the coffeepot; others—who weren't generally morning people—sat at the dining table and waited for their better halves to get coffee for them.

Harrison shook his head and slouched farther into his seat. Maybe, if he looked like he'd had a shitty night, they'd stay far away from him. They needed to. Hell, even Logan was here with Alina. Harrison didn't know if she'd moved in permanently or not, but she was damn close to it. One of the apartments was being fixed up for them. At this point, Levi was building married quarters, like on a military base.

Harrison snorted at that. Several people turned and looked at him questioningly. He glared at them.

Logan's eyebrows shot up. "Aren't you a bear this morning."

Harrison closed his eyes. As far as he was concerned, getting out couldn't happen soon enough. He should go for a ten-mile jog to work off some tension. He hadn't had a job that required a lot of skill in several weeks, and he was up for it. More to the point, he was rather desperate for something to happen.

Alfred appeared at that moment, looking a little more tired than usual. Harrison felt instant guilt. He'd been sitting on his butt, growling at the world, while Alfred could have used help in the kitchen. Harrison hopped up, walked into the kitchen and picked up the other platters of food. He brought them out and muttered as he passed Alfred, "Sorry, buddy. I should've been helping."

Alfred patted him on the shoulder. "Don't worry about it. There's adjustment needed here for everyone."

"Yeah, you're not kidding."

When breakfast was almost done, Ice's phone rang. "Hey, Dad. What's up?" Not long afterward she put down her fork and stiffened.

Levi turned to watch her. Silence descended on the table. Ice's father was a doctor who ran the private hospital in California where Levi, Rhodes, Merk and Stone went to recover when their very lives had been in danger almost a year before. Maybe it was over a year ago. Harrison couldn't even remember—it seemed so long ago. From the look on Ice's face, her father may be in trouble.

She got up and grabbed the remote to turn on the wall screen beside him. She pushed a few buttons, and her father appeared onscreen. "Go ahead, Dad. You're on video here while we all have breakfast."

Relief flooded his face when he saw her. "My night was a little rough. I'm sure you heard on the news yesterday about the senator being shot?"

"Yes, Senator Branson," Levi spoke up. "What's going on?"

"His wife is currently a patient in my hospital. She's an old friend, and she's in a bad way. It's hard to get the full story from her as she's been terribly hurt and is drifting in and out of consciousness. I'm not sure if she's withholding secrets, scared of bad press, fears for the safety of her family, or all of it. But the bottom line is, her daughter has gone missing. Actually the son has too, but that's not unusual. Anyway, so far nobody's had any luck locating the daughter. She's twenty-seven. Very smart. Did a stint in the military. She had some bad experience there, and when her time was up, walked away and didn't look back. Honestly … she's rumored to have shot her father. I've met her several times. If she *did*, I'm inclined to believe she had good reason. However, that's only a rumor."

Ice and Levi looked at each other, then at the screen.

Harrison leaned forward. "Richard, what about the relationship between the son and the senator?"

Ice's father nodded. "Hello, Harrison. Haven't seen you in a long time, buddy."

Harrison cracked a smile. "In my case, it's probably a good thing."

Richard smiled, then continued. "As far as the son, he's being groomed for a career in politics. He seems to be doing an outstanding job on his father's campaign trail to get him re-elected. He's eighteen months older than his sister. The siblings have never been close. Not lots of love between them. I'd say the opposite is true. But not enough that she'd abandon her brother. They are still siblings, and she's the more responsible one of the two."

"What happened to the mother?" Harrison asked. "Why is she in your hospital? Was she shot too?"

Richard shook his head. "No. She's been severely beaten. She's got bruises all over her face, neck, shoulders, and arms. It looks like she was on the ground and took several blows and kicks, even an attempted strangulation, while lying there. She's very slight, but she's tall. She's fifty-three and very lean. And, without much padding, her body suffered quite a beating."

"Is she conscious now? Can she talk to us?" Ice asked. "Because that's where we need to start."

"She's not coherent enough at this time."

Levi spoke up again. "Richard, I presume you're asking us to look for the daughter?"

Richard nodded. "Yes. The thing is, it has to be done quietly. I'd also like to know who beat up Trish. The local police are on this."

Levi sat back and crossed his arms. "Together? That can cause an awful lot of cross contamination and absolutely no sharing of information."

Richard tilted his head. "And I'm not even sure I can give you very much either."

Ice said, "Don't worry about it, Dad. We'll get what we can. Can you tell me when the daughter went missing and where the senator was shot?"

"The senator was shot at 7:15 p.m. last night on his doorstep. His wife arrived at my hospital shortly thereafter, and the daughter hasn't been seen since dinnertime."

"Any chance the gunman took the daughter?" Levi asked. "Or murdered and dumped her somewhere?"

Richard's face looked haggard as he contemplated the idea. "It's possible. And Ice, the reason Trish is here is because she called personally, asking me to help her."

"Have you told the police?" Levi asked, his voice hard. "Do you have any involvement in this case that'll turn up once we start digging?"

Richard shook his head. "I told the police she's here, under lock and key in intensive care, and badly beaten.

Other than that, I didn't tell them anything." He winced. "Trish didn't say much except that her daughter didn't hurt her. But it's possible the senator beat her up."

There was dead silence at the table.

Harrison shook his head and swore under his breath. Wife-beaters were very low on their list of men to help, and generally Legendary Security wouldn't work for them. But a senator who beat his wife? If that got out, well, that would create a media storm, and they'd have a harder time getting to the truth. "Why was she beaten as badly as she was? I guess the real question is, was the senator shot before or after?" Harrison studied Richard's face.

"We can't determine that yet. Both happened so closely together." Richard sighed, then glanced around the room and smiled. "Levi, I see a lot of new members on your team, and most are women. I like that."

"And that's a good thing," Ice said, her voice calm. "But they aren't necessarily all on the team. Dad, many of the team have partners now."

A faint smile crossed his lips as he nodded his head. "Good for them. I must get back to work. Is this something your team can help me with? Trish is afraid for her daughter."

Levi nodded.

At that Harrison jumped in the conversation again. "I can be on a plane within a couple hours."

Richard gave a heavy sigh. "Thank you. Stay at my house, Harrison. I have no idea where this trail will lead. But it could go across the country. This girl had military connections. I don't know what the hell she was into since leaving the service. If she did shoot the senator, maybe it was to stop him from killing Trish. She certainly has the training for it, and she's become a bit of a wild card. A lot of anger and I think hurt." He flashed a tired smile and shut down the video.

Harrison sat back and said, "Wow. A wife-beating senator." He leaned forward. "Is the senator dead or just shot?"

Everybody looked at each other to get confirmation.

"I believe he said 'shot.' I'm not sure that meant the senator has died. Yet. We'll follow up." Ice stood. "I'll head to the office to see what information I can find."

Sienna spoke from the far side of the table. "I'll make your travel arrangements, Harrison."

Levi turned to Harrison and said, "You're not going alone. Too often our cases go sideways."

Harrison rolled his eyes. "Well, throw in a couple of the new guys. Everyone else here is lovey-dovey." He said it in such a caustic tone, they all looked at him. He didn't give a shit.

As he walked away, he heard Levi explaining to the others how *Harrison has cabin fever and needs to get out for a bit.*

Under his breath, he muttered, "Yeah, that's putting it mildly."

He shouldn't take it out on them though. They were all happy, and that was the way life should be. So it wasn't their fault he sucked in the relationship department. His track record was all kinds of bad. That was why he wasn't ready to move forward. But he had come to terms with it.

In his own way.

Or he could always move off the compound and look for another job. He growled at the thought. But he was twisting himself up, down, and sideways living where he was now. It had been bearable until Logan and Alina moved in together. And yet he liked Alina, so that made no sense.

So, what the hell was this all about?

Sour grapes, said the little voice inside. *Jealousy. You know you don't want to be alone. But your chances of that ever changing aren't good, and you're afraid you could be the one single man in the compound who doesn't find somebody special.*

This time when he growled, he rolled his eyes. "Just perfect," he muttered.

Chapter 2

ZOE BRANSON SQUATTED on the street corner at Benji's side. His tin cup and white cane were before him as he played his faithful guitar. She'd been here for most of the morning. She should go grab them both a coffee. But now she was too lazy, tired, and happy, enjoying just sitting for a few minutes. It was hard to do anything other than that right now.

She was always looking over her shoulder. She had so much hate and anger inside her that she didn't know what to do anymore. She needed to pound someone into the ground, but she had nobody to use to do so. Besides, she'd found out that following through did her more harm than good. That was the facts of life.

"You don't have to sit here and keep me company, little one," Benji said. His fingers gently strummed the guitar.

A mother and child walked by. The boy dropped some coins into Benji's cup.

He smiled and said, "Bless you, child."

Zoe watched the boy walk away, his hand in his mom's, being carried along even as he kept an eye on Benji.

"How did you know it was a child?" she whispered.

"The footsteps."

She rolled her eyes and nodded. "How did you know that a child dropped the coin?"

"Because the lack of force with which the coins fell. And they didn't fall from far off the ground."

She chuckled. "Good answer. How about I grab us two coffees?" She stood. "Have you eaten today?"

His nod said absolutely. "I had an apple and half a sandwich this morning."

She checked her watch. It was almost two. "You got dinner plans, or are you happy with whatever I pick up?"

His laughter was rich as it rolled across the street. "I never turn down a meal, no matter if I got plans or not."

"Isn't that the truth?" She turned to add, "Back in ten."

"Maybe today you will. Probably tomorrow you won't."

He had been saying something similar off and on for the last few days. She realized she couldn't argue with him because she could pick up and leave without a moment's notice. For the present she was here. And that was the way she liked it. She was anonymous. Nobody knew who she was, where she came from, and nobody cared. At this moment, she was golden.

A block away was a coffee shop in the Riverside Center. Her diet sucked presently, but she didn't care. Her normal rations consisted of all-natural yogurt and lots of fresh veggies and fruit. When she hit the streets, it was amazing how easily she became accustomed to not having all the things she used to love. Especially when the penalty meant she had to take the shit that came with it. She couldn't do that right now. She might not be up for it ever again.

She briefly contemplated leaving the country, a daily thought in her mind. But…could she do that if her mother lived? Her mother was the only person she cared about. She knew others said she had been the one to beat up her mom. That was a lie. She was fully capable of beating somebody up, but never her mother, the one who'd been her protective buffer against the world. Her mother had warned her to walk away when she came up against some of the most horrible offenses in the military. Being a man and serving was one thing, as a woman it was a completely different story.

Her best friend had been raped by several men in their own unit. Such a horrible betrayal of both body and mind. Zoe had fought so hard to get justice. But when she found her friend hanging in the bathroom, tied up with her own shirt, she'd walked. There'd been no justice for her friend. None.

And she doubted it would happen in her lifetime. There were so many cover-ups. The military couldn't handle the thought that soldiers were anything but perfect. The men she'd believed to be good, honest, and upright patriots had turned on one of their own. And they were still raping other women.

A rock sat in her path. She pulled her leg back and kicked it as far as she could. She had enough anger sliding through her that it shot forward, bounced and kept on rolling. But it wasn't a big enough outlet for her temper.

She entered the coffee shop and ordered two. Picking them up, she walked to the store next door and checked out a couple sandwiches on the menu. It was cheaper if she bought a large quantity. Benji could pack one away for later, and she could too. She bought four large with everything and had them wrapped and bagged so she take them to-go.

With her purchases in hand, she made her way to where Benji sat. She'd seen him many times over the last few months since she'd left the military. In fact, when she needed to get away after her father's shooting, Benji had been the first man on her mind. And the lifestyle he lived. She'd followed his example and disappeared into the streets.

He was still singing, strumming away on his guitar, soulfully happy. She didn't understand how that could be. It seemed like life was against him, that he'd always gotten the wrong end of the stick. And nobody gave a damn. Yet every day he showed up with a smile on his face, a gentle ring of happiness around his heart, and cheerfully played his guitar for silver coins in his cup.

She needed to find some of that. She'd been sitting beside him, looking to see what his secret was. As it was right now, her anger was poisoning her. Eventually it would kill her. She was okay with that. Except she couldn't leave her mom alone and unprotected. That asshole who shot her father would come back. No way he wouldn't if he had intended to kill her father. The question dominant in her mind was, did he plan to take out her mom next? And was he alone or coming as part of a pack?

HARRISON'S FLIGHT WAS due to depart soon, and he had been allowed early boarding. He opened his laptop and downloaded the information Ice sent—personal histories, including military records of all the family members. Richard, Ice's father, would send his man Foster to the San Diego International Airport to meet Harrison when he landed and to drive him to Richard's place. That was good because Richard had one hell of a house. And Harrison was always up for living in some luxury. Besides, Richard lived alone. Harrison wouldn't have to deal with any romantic mess there.

He looked at the senator's file first. According to the reports, several death threats had been made against him, vicious letters delivered and nasty emails sent. Nothing the police had found was viable enough to convict anybody. The senator was well-loved within his constituency and yet hated by so many others. A strong religious faction had put him in power and shaped his own beliefs. He was antiabortion and antigun, yet he owned a firearm himself. In interviews, he gave confusing statements and countered questions with more questions. The media loved to hate him and vice versa. But nothing in here showed signs he had had a violent past or whispered he might've been a wife-beater.

For all intents and purposes, they were the perfect family—from the outside. The senator was born into money, and married into a wealthy family.

Harrison looked at the wife's file next. In comparison to her husband's, Trish's file was very slim. She had two children and spent most of her time doing charity work now that the son and daughter were older. Trish appeared to be well-loved by the community, was often a guest speaker for women's rights, and loved the underdog. No death threats against her personally, but there were some in association with her husband. She'd been born into big money and had been groomed to marry it as well.

The kids had gone to boarding and private schools their whole lives, making Harrison wonder how they had any relationship as a family while spending so much time apart. Yet the comments made by those who knew Trish were how caring a mother she was and how involved she was in her children's lives. Of course, those were surface observations. Who knew what the truth was? They had live-in servants: a housekeeper and a man who doubled as the gardener and chauffeur. Harrison shrugged. He couldn't imagine what Trish's days were like.

Harrison pulled out the next file. The son had followed in his father's footsteps: top-notch universities that led to some business experience and now into politics. He was not as well-loved, or as well-hated, as his father, but he was still young and could fall either way with time. He was a ladies' man. Ice had included a picture of him in a tuxedo. On each arm, he was escorted by a beautiful woman. He looked like it was his right in life. Yet a bit of tension was around his lips. And the look in his eyes was not necessarily one Harrison was particularly fond of. *Arrogance.* Like some, he had been born with a silver spoon in his mouth and fully expected everybody else to cater to him.

But then what could one expect from a rich pretty boy who never had to do a real day's work in his life?

When Harrison opened the daughter's file, he found only a few pages but slowed his reading. Something about her really caught his attention. Nothing Richard had said gave any indication as to what was going on in her world. They also didn't know if she had been kidnapped and possibly murdered as a result of the earlier attacks on her parents. She'd done a stint in the military, joining against her parents' wishes. Apparently they had quite a fight over it, but she was an adult, and with her thumb to her nose, had joined anyway.

She'd done her time, and then she'd walked. She was a top-notch martial arts expert. And although she'd been training since she was young, and on the surface she'd been given every advantage, she didn't appear to like team sports. Throughout her childhood she had attended classes in shooting, archery, martial arts, and of course, all the expected "refined" curriculum, like painting and music. Yet she had turned to the military anyway—the ultimate in team sports.

And there she had excelled. She had a competitive edge, and maybe, finally throwing off the shackles of her family, had found a place of her own.

Until something changed. Harrison read through lots of glowing recommendations and comments about her behavior—top of the class, strong with teamwork, and dependable. But as he read farther, he noted a dividing line, separating the time *before* and *after.* Some inciting incident had warranted the comments afterward. *Angry. Undisciplined. No respect for authority.* She was recommended for a psych evaluation. Turned it down. Was forced to attend. Showed up, then walked out. He raised his eyebrows at that. It took a lot to thumb her nose at the military. That was one hell of a big machine to buck. When it stomped back, a lot of people got hurt. He didn't know what had gone on in her world, but something had.

From top of the class to the bottom of the ranks mentally, emotionally, and physically. She appeared to have stopped caring or wanted out so badly she'd do anything. But the military wasn't very good at letting people leave.

He kept reading but found little more, and nothing that explained her current behavior. He was more fascinated than ever. For all intents and purposes, she was well-loved but had probably found the authority too much to bear. Her father couldn't have been easy to live with. And growing up in the public eye was never fun.

If she hadn't had the beauty of her mother, that could've been an issue as well. Her brother, Alex, appeared to be the favored child, and that would've been another. Harrison wanted to label her the poor little rich girl, but there was something about the look in her eyes in her first military photo—where she looked so damn proud and happy—that he couldn't do anything but smile. He remembered his initial military days too. He knew exactly how she felt.

Then there was a second picture—her exit photo as she walked out, filled with anger, a tight pinched look to her lips and a hardened gaze. *No. Not anger. Violence was in her now.* He shook his head. "What happened to you?"

She'd be twenty-seven, going on twenty-eight. And, since leaving the military, nobody had any idea what she was up to other than floating through life. She stayed in touch with the family but had no permanent job. According to reports, she'd been home that day her father had been shot. But the time line was confused. Nobody knew how long she'd been there, where she'd come from, or if she'd walked in, shot her father and walked out. He studied the exit photo. The look in her eyes. With that anger, she absolutely would have no trouble shooting her father and running—if he was her target. But Harrison doubted she had. Something had occurred during those years in the military, but something else a few years later for her father to end up with a bullet in his head and her mother beaten and in a private hospital.

Harrison closed the folders and shut down his laptop as the stewardesses came around with drinks. He stared out the window, wondering what the hell had happened to that "perfect" family. Bad circumstances didn't seem to care how much money anybody had.

Shit happened to them all.

He landed at the airport to see Foster, Richard's man, waiting for him. Traveling was so much easier when walking out of a massive airport, Harrison could find a friendly face. As he got to the limousine, he opened the front door, getting in the passenger's side.

"It's good to see you, Foster." Harrison smiled at him.

"It's good to see you too, sir. You're alone, right? How are you?"

"I'm meeting two of the guys in Coronado. But I'll be staying at Richard's place."

"It'll be good to have another face around the table. Richard's been very busy lately. It's been pretty quiet at the house."

Harrison could imagine.

"Still, it's a big place, and there's always work to be done." Foster chuckled. "I happen to like yard work. And the house makes me happy." He shot a glance at Harrison. "I've been there going on twenty years now, you know?"

"Wow. You must be happy then."

"Indeed. I moved into the cottage a couple years ago. That's made for a nice change too."

Harrison leaned back against the seat and settled in for the drive through the heavy traffic. There were a lot worse things in life than having your own little cottage in a ritzy place like that.

"Richard isn't around enough to cause any work. If the house functions and stays safe and secure while he's gone, he's happy."

"But who's cooking?" Harrison asked. "And how is Richard's health and attitude lately?"

Foster seemed to stiffen a bit.

"I'm only asking because Ice is concerned."

Foster relaxed. "It would be nice to see her again."

"Like Richard, she's busy. They are two peas in a pod. They went in opposite directions, but they're both filling their lives by doing a lot of good for many people."

"A man can't ask for any more of his kids than that,"

Foster said.

Harrison thought about it. Nobody at the compound had any, nor were any of the women pregnant or already a mother. He couldn't imagine what that would do to the place when they did. Surely that was the next step. How could it not be? Whether it was a good thing or not, he wasn't at all sure.

When they reached Richard's driveway, they found the lights on and a car parked out front. "Richard's home."

Harrison hopped out, grabbed his bag from the back seat and walked to the front door. It opened, and there was Richard. He was tired and a little frailer than the last time Harrison saw him. Although Richard visited Ice when he could, and Ice made a point to see him as often as she could, the rest of the guys didn't see Richard much.

"You should move to Texas," Harrison said. "We could always use a doctor on the compound."

Richard laughed. "Maybe, if grandchildren become a possibility, I'll consider it," he said, "but I'm not ready to retire yet."

His comment was in line with what Harrison had wondered about earlier—children at the compound—and he smiled. "That would be something to see. I can't imagine Ice having children."

"Oddly enough, I can. When she was growing up, she was always babysitting the neighbors' kids. It will happen one day. But hopefully not for a while. I am not quite ready for that stage of life either."

Richard showed Harrison to his room. Harrison dropped his bag next to the bed and followed Richard to the living area. "Any change in Trish's condition?"

Richard shook his head. "No."

There was something in his voice, then a whisper of emotion ran across his face that had Harrison wondering what was going on between those two. As Richard handed him a brandy, and they sat in front of the fireplace, Harrison had to ask, "How well do you know Trish?"

"We were in a relationship before she married the senator." He swirled brandy around in his glass. "At the time I was doing my residency, and that was tough enough to get through without finding hours in my day for a woman who was fairly demanding. At least I thought she was back then. I wasn't making the money she wanted, so she married up."

"Not an uncommon story," Harrison murmured.

"No, not at all." Richard smiled. "But life experience makes one change perspectives. As I look back over those years, I realized that, as much as I'd like to return to those days, maybe give her more attention to keep her in my life, it was not to be."

"And if her husband passes away?"

Richard raised his gaze and laughed. "She's been married thirty years. One doesn't walk away easily from something like that."

"Did her husband beat her?"

Richard sucked in a deep breath and let it out slowly. "I don't know for sure. I've seen her a few times over the past dozen years. There were never any visible bruises. Yet she'd recoil if someone made a sudden movement or easily startled if approached from behind. The signs of abuse were there. However, the beating she sustained this time almost brutalized her face, the feminine elegance she had. If I didn't know better, I'd say a woman had done it."

Chapter 3

As Zoe returned to Benji's side, he sat in silence. He wasn't playing; he wasn't singing. And the look on his face had turned tense. She glanced around, but didn't see anything wrong. "Benji, it's me."

He inclined his head and said, "I know it is, girl. You need to walk right past."

She froze. "Why is that?"

"Footsteps stopped just outside of my hearing," he whispered in low tones. "They've been standing there for a good seven to eight minutes."

She placed a cup of coffee in front of him, took a sandwich from her bag and placed it in front of him, then said, "One coffee, one sandwich."

"God bless you, child. Now go. Whoever it is, they're on the far side of the street." He reached out, found the coffee cup with his hand and picked it up. "Now that they found you, make sure you don't come back."

She straightened and, with a heavy heart, took the other coffee out of its cardboard carrier. A trash receptacle was up ahead. She dumped the cardboard tray and kept going. At the intersection, she stopped, looked at the lights and casually glanced around the neighborhood. Indeed, somebody was on the far side, dressed in jeans, a black T-shirt and hoodie—the hood not on his head—with dark sunglasses and a baseball cap.

She snorted out loud. "Like he doesn't stand out." Several people stopped at the intersection with her. When the lights changed to cross the road, she turned in the direction of the man upsetting Benji. She didn't know who the hell he was after, but she planned to get a good look at him. And if he was after her, he wouldn't find her easy prey. She'd learned a long time ago to take the offensive instead of waiting for someone to come after her.

She didn't recognize the man at all. But that didn't mean much. He could be hired muscle. She also didn't know if he was connected to either her father's shooting or her mother's beating.

As he watched her coming toward him, he straightened and shifted back farther. But his eyes were those of a predator.

She was no man's prey.

She looked at the hot coffee in her hand. She really wanted to enjoy it, not waste it by having to throw it at him. She glanced around for other options. She wasn't very good on that whole idea of *ignoring things in life*. She already had evidence of that. She lowered the bag with the sandwiches along her far side. As she walked closer, she slipped the bag over her wrist and lifted the lid off the coffee. She could almost hear Benji on the other side of the street saying, "Don't do it, girlie. Don't do it."

She walked up to the stranger and said, "Making sure you aren't here to cause trouble."

He stepped back and raised his hands. "Whoa, crazy lady. I'm not doing anything."

She smiled. "Yeah, you better believe it. Get the hell out of here and don't come back. You've got three seconds to move, or you'll have this boiling hot coffee all over you."

Instead of taking off, he got ugly and stepped forward. "I don't take orders from you."

She didn't give him three seconds before the hot coffee went fully in his face. As he screamed, she turned and walked past, deliberately giving him her back. That added to the insult of being bested by a woman. She tossed the empty cup in another trash bin and strolled on, as if not giving a damn.

At the church up ahead, she sat on the steps, pulled out one of her sandwiches and proceeded to take a bite. She could see him rubbing his face and swearing. She was a good fifty yards away. But she'd made him. Benji had too. And how interesting was that? Blind and yet he could still spot trouble. She owed him one.

Something she couldn't afford to let happen again. Assholes like this guy … well, the world was a better place without them. As she munched away at her sandwich, a stranger walked up and sat beside her. He had two cups of coffee in his hands. He held one out.

She stared at it and then at him. No alarm bells went off. Not yet anyway. "Aren't you afraid I'll throw that at you?"

"If you really feel you should. However, as I mean you no harm, why would you?"

She glared at him. But dammit, she wanted that coffee. She took it, popped off the top and realized it was black—the way she liked it. "Who the hell are you?"

"The name's Harrison. I work for Legendary Security."

She froze. "Isn't that Levi's company?"

Startled, he turned to face her, his huge blue eyes staring at her.

Eyes completely at odds with the rest of him.

He shook his head. "How do you know Levi's group?"

"Don't know them. Heard of them."

He nodded once. "Levi's done well."

She curled her lip. "So they say. Doesn't mean I believe everything I hear."

"Good thing." He took the lid off his cup. It was black too.

She set hers between her legs and proceeded to finish her sandwich. She glanced at the man she'd attacked. He remained against the wall, glaring at her. Why was he still here? He had to be waiting for somebody. No other reason for him to stay put at this point. The game was up. She glanced around to see who might have come to his aid, realizing it could easily be the man beside her. "You with him?"

He chuckled. "Hell, no. If it had been me, you'd never see me coming."

"Is that why you approached me here? So while my attention was on him, you could sneak up on the other side?"

He shook his head. "Levi doesn't hire fools. Has no time for failures."

"Well, we agree on something," she muttered.

"What the hell is Zoe Branson doing on the streets and using a blind man as an alarm system?"

She stiffened. She didn't know who the hell this Harrison was, but that he knew her name had her already contemplating her options. She could run straight across the street, disappear in the alley on the far side. But he looked fit and quite possibly could outrun her.

She could throw the hot coffee in his face and bolt, but she figured he'd probably run after her and catch her before she was gone. She could pull a few martial arts tactics, jump the railing and bolt, but she suspected he had a few of his own. She stared at the last bite of sandwich left in her hand. It tasted like sawdust now. Deciding she needed the energy anyway, she finished it, chewing long and hard, then looked at the sandwich still in her bag. "Who the hell are you really?"

"I'm really Harrison. And I really work for Legendary Security."

"How did you track me down, and why the hell do you give a damn?"

"Not sure I do. I get paid either way."

His tone was aloof, but humor threaded through it. She took umbrage at the latter. She had had nothing to laugh at in so long …

"Besides, I didn't have much problem finding you. It's what I do, and I'm damn good at it."

She was prepared to blast him again when he turned, piercing her with those blue eyes and said, "And I'm here really for your mother's sake."

That shut her up. God she'd been panicked to find out about her mother's condition. How could this man know? And could she believe him? "How is she?"

"In and out of consciousness. I understand the damage is severe but not life-threatening."

"I don't even know where she is," she whispered, pain in her tone. She had to watch out for those kinds of emotion. The last thing she wanted was for anybody to know her mom was her weakness.

He held out his hand, palm up. "I can take you to see her if you want."

She stared at that hand and wondered at herself. She was contemplating placing her hand in his. But that would signify trust. That was like holding out an olive branch and having somebody accept it. Everything was symbolic about this. He was asking a lot of her. The stranger seemed to know so much about her, and she knew nothing of him.

With childlike movements, she put her hands on the step and sat on them. He laughed out loud. And she knew he understood exactly what she'd done and why.

But he left his hand where it was and said, "Whenever you're ready."

"Hell, no." She shook her head. "I'm no fool."

"You're not, but you are in trouble."

"Am not."

The corner of his mouth twitched, and in a singsong voice, he matched her words with "Am too."

She sagged in place. "I can't go. Someone might follow me there and hurt her. Nobody can know where I am."

"I didn't say anybody would know where you were going. I offered to take you to see your mom."

"And then what?"

"I can return you to these church steps if that's what you want."

"Like I trust you."

His smile, when it came, was slow and sweet. "You should trust somebody. You can't be alone for the rest of your life."

"Can to," she snapped, right back into that childish voice.

He chuckled. "You could try. But it's not who you are. A lot of anger is inside you. Maybe even hatred. Not too sure what happened to make you who you are today, but the woman from a few years ago, she wasn't about being alone. She wasn't about forging her own path, kicking tires along the way. That one, she was more about globetrotting around the world and finding beaches, sunshine, and palm trees—maybe dancing with the wind, a flower in your hair."

She stared at him in surprise. "What the hell do you know about who I was and am?"

"I've read a file on you."

"You haven't seen the whole file," she said with a disgusted snort.

"Nope, I haven't. But I can read between the lines. You were military. Happily ensconced in a world where you excelled. The top of your class and could thumb your nose at your father—a man you did your best to get away from all your life." He turned his head to stare at her. "How am I doing so far?"

Her response was to cross her arms over her chest and lean against the steps' railing. In a disaffected tone she said, "So what? You can read a file. What you see now is the unhappy rich bitch. You don't know me. You don't know anything about me."

"I know an injustice was done. I know you couldn't fight whatever it was that happened. I don't know if it was somebody close to you or something that happened to you. But you were forever changed by the incident." His tone was low and compassionate. "It was major. Traumatic. And at the time, you felt completely alone. You're still in the angry stage. If you keep this up, soon you will be into the depression stage. Depression is anger that has no outlet."

"How do you know I'm not already there?" she snapped, hating the fear sparking inside her. How did he so quickly come to understand who she was and what she was doing? She didn't even know how to react. So much anger was inside her, boiling, going nowhere.

His gaze narrowed as he studied her. And then he

seemed to decide. He stood with his coffee in one hand, and with his other still open in a nonthreatening yet insistent way, he said, "Let's walk."

She shook her head.

"This isn't the time to play games. Your friend is about to get company."

"I don't give a shit," she said in a low, mean voice. "You can go back to wherever the hell you came from. Leave me alone. I'll take care of those assholes. Don't you worry."

He nodded. "I believe you. But at some point, you could be outnumbered. And that time is now."

She narrowed her gaze, passed a sidelong look to the man she threw her coffee at. Sure enough, there were four of them now. They were all big—mean and tough thugs. She assessed her situation and realized she was in deep shit.

In a voice that brooked no argument, he said, "Now."

She stood but ignored his hand.

"I highly suggest you look like you are with me and not against me. Because they're approaching us right now."

Instinctively she grabbed his hand. And he helped her down the last of the steps. As they turned to leave, she said, "We can't run. If we do, we'll always be running."

He faced her, his eyebrows raised. "You already are. How does this change anything?"

She frowned and walked at his side. She didn't want to assess what he had just said. But the truth lingered in the air.

Several yards ahead of them, two more big men peeled away from a parking lot and stepped toward the sidewalk.

She froze, but Harrison nudged her gently forward. "Those are my men."

Instinctively she could feel her heart and mind relaxing—wanting to accept this as normal. Was this a good thing? Considering four men were behind her, it was a very good thing. Now the odds were even. And she'd put her money on Harrison any day.

She assessed the two men in front of her. One with hair so damn blond it was pure white and the other had that thin tensile strength to him. He was lean, but he had that mean kick-somebody-into-the-ground look on his face. They were both tall. And though she used the word *lean*, in no way were these men skinny.

"What do you guys eat anyway? You all sure are huge." She couldn't keep the resentful tone out of her voice. Years of taking abuse from everybody around her, especially in the military, had given her a good understanding of how much size gave people an edge. And she didn't have it.

Harrison chuckled and said, "On any given day, anything we see."

"I believe it." She wanted to turn her head and check out the guys behind him.

"Don't bother. They're still following. They'll stop as soon as we meet up with these two."

As they approached, both men nodded at Harrison, then turned their gaze on her. As they arrived at the same spot, Harrison's men peeled off and split, one to either side of Harrison and Zoe, so they were walking four in a row.

She snorted. "Yeah, okay, so that's testosterone times three."

Harrison gently squeezed her fingers and said, "It is what it is. You can beat up Mother Nature all you want. It won't change anything. You're still female, and that does come with some physical limitations."

"Doesn't mean I have to take it easy," she muttered. She wondered why the only *perfect* males were *perfect* assholes.

"What's the matter? Always wanted to be Daddy's boy?"

"As if. Besides, he already has one of those."

"You know you sound like a disgruntled child, right?"

"Then you're not so smart," she snapped. Before she realized it, she'd been led to a Jeep. Not a military, but a modern black four-door civilian kind. "I thought only yuppie women used this vehicle for their kids now. Hardly seems like something you guys would drive."

"Be nice." Harrison opened the passenger door. "Get in."

She stuck out her jaw. "And if I don't?"

One of the men beside them took a step forward. She spun and took a fighting stance. "Just try it."

Harrison gave a small sigh. "Later today I'll go a few good rounds with you so you can work out some of that temper. But preferably in a dojo or weight room. These men are not here to hurt you."

She slowly straightened and shot him an uncertain look, then using her hands, climbed into the passenger seat.

He slammed the door shut and raised his eyes to the other two. "I'll drive. You guys sit in the back." He walked around to the driver's seat, opened the door, hopped in and turned on the engine.

"Where did the other four assholes go?"

"Into the gutter," he said quietly. "Don't worry. If they show up again, we'll deal with them."

"You know who they are?"

"Hired muscle. But other than that, no. And no, I don't know who hired them or what they want you for."

"I do," she whispered. "If it comes to that, I'll kill them before they take me alive."

HARRISON FROZE AT her words. He turned in his seat to study her face. From the set look in her eyes and her squared-off jaw, he knew she meant every word. "It won't come to that."

She glared at him. "But if it does …"

"Then I'll shoot every one of them. But I will do it, not you."

He popped the Jeep into reverse. He could hear her spluttering beside them. He knew the men in the back found her quite interesting too. But then, she wasn't one of the most normal of females either. She worked to appear damn hard. But she was terrified. Once he had realized that, he'd overlooked all the rest.

He knew his way to Richard's hospital. He'd been one of the guards looking after Levi way back when. But Harrison still needed to let Richard know ahead of time. He quickly sent a text, pulled into traffic and, in case they were being followed, took a very meandering route.

When they pulled into the rear of the hospital and parked in the private parking area, there was no sign anybody had tried to follow them. He got out, waited 'til she hopped down, and came around and said, "While we're here, you don't say anything to anybody. Understand?"

She gave him an uncertain look, then a clipped nod. "Why is my mom here? In a private hospital?"

"Because she has friends, good friends. One of them pulled some strings."

"Oh," she said in a small voice. "Good for her."

He took her to the rear entrance. He had the code for the door. But it would be changed either before he left or the end of the day. He also knew security would be aware he'd come in and their cameras would be on them right now.

He led the way to the small elevator at the back, brought it into service, and the four of them got in. He pushed the button to take them to the third floor. When it opened, two men stood at the side. Harrison nodded at them, and they nodded in return.

Zoe stared in fear. "How bad is she? Why is she under guard?"

"You know the answer to that last one."

She fell silent.

She was doing her best to stay strong and stand firm, but he doubted she had any idea just how damaging all this was to her psych.

As he approached the room on the left, Richard stepped forward from the main desk on the far side. He nodded and said, "Hello, Zoe."

She looked up at him and asked, "Do I know you?"

Richard smiled. "It's been a few years. I'm a friend of your mom's."

Understanding whispered across her face. "You're the doctor?" She turned to Harrison. "You're right. My mom does have good friends." She turned to Richard and smiled. "It has been a long time. Thank you very much for looking after my mother."

"The pleasure is all mine. I'm sorry she's in such a state. And that's why I need to see her before you go in." He quickly explained about her mother's condition. "I don't know that she is cognizant or that she'll recognize your voice. It's important she not be upset. And she is my patient, under my care. For that reason, Harrison and I will go into the room with you. If you cause a disturbance, he will pick you up and haul you out." His gaze narrowed as he added, "Do you understand me?"

She nodded. "I would never do anything to hurt my mother."

He studied her for a long moment and then nodded. "I believe you, but we don't always know if we'll hurt somebody with our words. And that's why it's very important she not be upset."

Harrison watched as she wiped her damp palms on her pants and felt the fear emanate from her. He took her arm. "Almost ready?"

She took a deep breath and nodded, then watched as the other two guys with Harrison took up posts on either side of her mother's door.

Richard opened the door and stepped in, shutting the door softly behind him. A moment later he let the two of them in. She could hear the beeps of the monitors in the quiet room. Unlike most, this one was more like a sitting room. There was, indeed, a hospital bed, but it had bright colored blankets and a couch off to one side, with a big picture window filled with flowers. Even a nice little throw rug had been placed on the floor beside her mom's bed for her bare feet to touch, should she wake and wish to move about.

But then Zoe's gaze landed on her mother. She gasped out loud, her hand clamping over her lips to hold back her cry. Harrison watched as the tears came to the corners of her eyes.

And, like Harrison thought, she'd just confirmed she had not been responsible for her mother's beating. Richard might have worried that a woman had done this—and that was still a possibility—but it certainly wasn't by Zoe's hand.

She stood and stared for a long moment and then slowly stepped forward to look at her mom. In a surprise move, she dropped to her knees and rested her cheek against her mom's arm.

A poignant moment.

Knowing it would be okay to leave the two of them alone in the room with Trish, Richard gave Harrison a quiet smile of thanks and stepped outside.

Harrison stood watch. And wondered. What had brought these two women to this unbelievable low in their lives?

Chapter 4

ZOE LIFTED HER head, leaned over, kissed her mom gently on her cheek and whispered, "Stay strong, Mom. I'll be back." She stepped away, brushing the tears from her eyes, and left her mother's room, passing Harrison's two sentries just outside.

Harrison walked out the door with her. In the hallway, she searched for the ladies' room, found it on the left near her mom's room and headed straight for it. She checked to see if Harrison followed her, but he remained outside her mom's door, talking to his two men. Seeing her mom like that—broken, bruised, and nonresponsive—had been heartbreaking.

Her mother had always been there for her. She might not have had the answers Zoe wanted, but her mom always had a hug and a kind word. It'd been frustrating at times, because when Zoe had wanted action, her mom was all about acceptance. Her mom kept saying how she'd already seen so much in life that nothing surprised her anymore. How she didn't like it, but one couldn't fight some things. And that was true enough. But Zoe also knew one had to fight other things because the alternative was too devastating.

In the bathroom, Zoe quickly washed her face, blew her nose and then used the facilities. After washing her hands, she stared into the mirror, thinking of what had been going on with her family. Harrison had nailed it when he had said she was on the run. Because she was. Running to get away from her life. Running to get away from her past. Running to get away from her family. And look what happened. She bowed her head, feeling the tears coming on yet again. She wanted to go in one of the stalls, curl up and cry.

But, if she didn't leave the restroom in a timely manner, she knew for a fact, Harrison would walk in and open every stall until he found her. He was like this indomitable presence. She didn't know where he came from. Sure, it was easy to say Legendary Security. Whatever the hell that meant. And he was hired to find her. If so, why? She straightened her shoulders, glared at her image in the mirror and whispered, "Well, it's damn time you found out."

She stiffened her hands into fists and strode from the bathroom. And all the stuffing went out of her as soon as she saw Richard.

He turned to look at her, and with that gentle smile said, "I'm sorry she wasn't awake for you, Zoe."

Instantly she was that little girl, back again in her mother's arms. She nodded mutely. "May I come see her again?"

Richard nodded. "Of course you can. But because of the security around here, we do need to know ahead of time."

"May I get your number so I can call to let somebody know?"

He pulled out his wallet, reached inside and grabbed a card for her. "Call me. I can set up whatever you need at the time."

"Thank you."

Harrison stepped beside her, gently wrapped an arm around her shoulder and said, "Thanks for letting us come in, Richard."

"It's definitely the best thing for Trish too. Maybe next time she'll be awake." With a gentle smile, he turned and walked to his small office.

Harrison led Zoe to the elevator, his two men once again stepping into place behind them. She wanted to insult them, to send them away, to get rid of the feeling they were here to protect her. Because that was what it felt like. And she didn't care it. As a matter of fact, she hated it. But at the same time, it worried her. Did she need their protection?

Or were they about stopping her from leaving, taking her somewhere she didn't want to go? She might be up to fighting one of them, but she couldn't fight all three. They looked to be damn good at what they did. And she had no doubt that was something she didn't want them to do.

Outside she took a deep breath and said, "When do I get to leave my prison?"

Harrison turned to face her. When she refused to look at him, he lifted her chin so she was forced to.

She glared, wishing she could hit him but knew it would go the wrong way for her.

"Have I ever indicated that you aren't smart?"

"Not in so many words," she said drily.

His gaze twinkled at her. "Then maybe you can relax a little bit."

She shook her head. "You know how long it's been since I could?"

"Who is it you're afraid of?"

She clammed up and stared, her face now poker straight.

He sighed. "Back to that trust issue."

She shrugged.

He motioned at the Jeep. "Where do you want to go?"

"Back to where you picked me up."

He looked like he wanted to argue.

"You said I'm not a prisoner," she snapped.

He gave in with a sigh. "Fine, let's go."

She didn't trust him, yet she took a seat in the front of the Jeep and waited. Again his two men, silent as always, slipped into the back. The trip was much faster this time, making her realize Harrison had taken a long and winding route getting to the hospital. If they had been followed, nobody succeeded. So, whatever. She could only deal with so many things at once. She'd tell Benji how she had to move on, now with four thugs after her, but that she'd get food and coffee to him somehow.

Harrison literally drove up to the church steps and parked. "Here you go."

She gave him a disbelieving look, opened the door and hopped out. She quickly closed it.

The Jeep didn't move; the men talked inside.

She shook her head. She couldn't leave until those guys did. Then she considered her sandwich bag. She sat again and looked at it. She wasn't hungry. But she needed fuel for sustenance, so she should eat now. But what she wanted to do was have the men disappear.

When the Jeep drove away, she sighed with relief. As she glanced up, her relief turned to anger. Harrison closed the distance and sat beside her on the steps. He motioned at the sandwich and asked, "Are you going to eat that?"

She opened her mouth and snapped it shut, then muttered, "Maybe."

"I figured it was for Benji."

She stiffened. "You better stay away from Benji," she warned.

He raised one eyebrow. "Have I hurt you? What makes

you think I would Benji?"

She slumped in place but didn't answer.

"You know, I think you've been looking at the world as an enemy for too long. You don't know how to tell who is a friend anymore."

"So? Are you a friend now?"

"I could be. But you're quite the clinical porcupine. If you aren't fed, it's like getting scratched by a feral cat."

For some reason that hurt. "That's not fair."

"No, it probably isn't," he said calmly. "I think, when you finally do decide that somebody is your friend, you defend them to your death if necessary. But you won't let anybody close because you're afraid to get hurt."

Startled, she looked at him again. "Are you some kind of shrink now?"

He shook his head. "No, but I was in the military for a lot of years. I saw things that could break anybody's heart and soul. I'm out now. But the world hasn't changed. Neither have the people."

She thought of all the things she knew about the military, and then all she'd seen since she'd left it and realized he was right. "Sometimes I hate people."

"Absolutely. But then we should be specific about those we hate."

"I haven't gotten very specific yet."

"That's the heart talking. That's the anger looking for an outlet. If you can cast a wide net, you're more likely to find somebody to beat up or to knock down so you feel justified hurting them. Set anger has an avenue, a path, a goal. But when you really look, you'll see—most likely—good people. And you can't justify hurting them."

"You don't know anything about me." She jumped to

her feet and walked along the street, her footsteps hard and rapid. But he was bigger than she was, his legs way longer than hers. He caught up with no trouble. "Go away."

"Nope, won't do that."

She came to a halt and turned to face him. "Why not? Why are you still with me? What do you want?"

"The truth. And then maybe some cooperation." His face was grim.

She glared at him suspiciously. "The truth about what? And what do you want my cooperation with?"

"You can push as hard as you want. You can be as mean and nasty as you want. You can be as prickly as a cactus. I don't really care, but you can't push me away."

Frustrated and angry, she spun on Harrison. The sandwich bag bashed against her thigh.

"You know, you can give that sandwich to Benji, and we could go somewhere nice to have a meal."

She snorted and continued down the street.

"We can also go to a friend's house, and you could have your own room and a shower, potentially grab some clean clothes if you have any. Someplace where you'll be safe while you sort this out."

She shook her head. "There won't be any sorting this out."

"Somebody hunting you?"

Her back stiffened, but she wouldn't give an answer.

"And is it the same person who shot your father and beat up your mother?"

She gasped and walked faster than ever. She was almost running.

He jerked her arm, making her stop. "If you want to go for a run that's fine, but I'd really rather put on my sneakers first. If you want to take on a 10 or 20K, I'm up for it. I haven't done a twenty in quite a while, but I could use the exercise."

She was panting now and didn't know what to say, except, "Leave me alone."

His voice softened, and he stroked her cheek. "I'm afraid that can't happen."

She looked up at him, her bottom lip trembling. She bit down on it hard and then whispered, "Why?"

He gave her that sweet smile again and said, "Because … I'm not sure I can."

AND HOW THE hell had that happened? He understood her disbelief. Hell, he was right there with her. His job had been to find her. That he'd done. But leaving her…that was something he couldn't force himself to do.

Is this what his friends had gone through? He had taken one look and in less than an hour, realized he was in trouble. He thought it was supposed to happen slowly, build on original lust and passion, good friendship. He didn't know what the hell he was feeling right now. He didn't know what to call it. He couldn't believe there was a name for this. But as he stood there and stared at her, he'd realized what he had said was quite true.

He couldn't make himself leave her.

She opened her mouth and snapped it closed again. After shooting him a fulminating look, she stepped back and said, "I don't understand."

Always one to be honest and upfront, he nodded. "Neither do I."

He looked around, people walking up and down the

street, more homeless claiming their quarters. The business day over, the evening starting. "I suggest we find a place to sit and have a hot meal. Take that sandwich to Benji and move forward."

She studied Harrison for a long moment, then nodded slowly. "But just dinner," she warned in a hard voice.

He gave her as gentle a smile as he could manage. "I'm not known for beating up girls, abusing women or doing anything with them against their will."

Her shoulders slumped. "I'm making too much of this, aren't I?"

He shook his head. "No. You should do what you're comfortable with."

"Okay then," she said as calmly as she could. "I don't want to waste this sandwich. So, you're right. Let's give it to Benji." Together they crossed the street and walked down the block to where the blind man sat, gently strumming his guitar.

"Glad it all worked out, girlie."

She laughed. "Well, it has for the moment. It's still early yet." She laid the bag with the sandwich against his knee. "Another sandwich for you. This guy will take me out for dinner."

Benji tilted his head and stared directly at Harrison. Then he nodded sagely. "You'll be safe with him."

Harrison crossed his arms over his chest and watched and waited.

She leaned forward and kissed Benji gently on the temple. "I'll see you tomorrow."

Benji shook his head. "Maybe you will, and maybe you won't."

She straightened and nodded at Harrison. They walked

on again. At the end of the next block she asked, "Where are we going?"

"We can go out for dinner, or to Richard's place for a meal."

"Oh, no. That would be imposing too much."

"I figured you'd say that," he said. "What about that steakhouse there?"

"Steak? I haven't had it in ages."

"Any particular reason?"

"Money," she said simply.

"And here I thought you were a rich girl," he mocked.

"When your life completely flips around, you don't waste money on unfruitful frivolities like a steak dinner. Sandwiches make your money go a whole lot further. Without knowing if I would get a job, or where I would live, I couldn't blow it like that. I had to save it all."

"Understood."

They walked in silence until they came to the steakhouse entrance.

He held the door open for her. She looked at her dirty leggings and T-shirt and winced. "They might not let me in."

"Then we'll find another place."

He stepped up to the hostess and asked for a table for two. The hostess smiled at him and seemed not to even notice what Zoe wore. That last part worked for him.

When they were seated at a booth by the window, he looked at her and smiled. "You worried for nothing."

"No," she said. "The hostess was under your spell. She never once glanced at me."

He chuckled. "Whatever works."

Their server came around with menus and asked if they

wanted anything to drink. They both refused and ordered dinner. Silence once again fell between them.

He could tell she was avoiding talking to him. She stared at the rest of the patrons, looked over the large floor, watched the comings and goings of the staff. He sat and waited. He'd been playing this game a lot longer than she had.

She glanced at him and in an irritable voice asked, "Why are you staring at me?"

"Because I like to."

He wanted to laugh when her glare deepened.

His phone rang. "Excuse me. I need to take this." He stood and walked to the washrooms so he could have a little more privacy and not disturb the other patrons. "Levi, what's up?"

"That's basically what I'm asking you. Saul and Dakota checked in. Said they left you downtown. On the church steps. And followed you to a restaurant?"

Harrison said, "Yep, they sure did. I'm with her now. Took her out for dinner. She's looking on the starved, lost, and lonely side. I think she's been on the run since she left her house. She still isn't talking. So I'm short on answers for her behavior. I did get her to the hospital so she could see her mom. No way she's responsible for her mother's injuries."

Levi gave a heavy sigh of relief. "Well, that's one good thing."

"Any updates?"

"Only that the father's condition has been downgraded yet again. They're worried about brain injury."

"Any word on the brother?" Harrison asked.

"No. Have you mentioned him to her at all?"

"No. She's really angry, but underneath all that, is fear.

I'm not sure why she's running or what from."

"Time to find out." Levi hung up.

Easy for Levi to say. Harrison put away his phone and walked back to his seat. This was hardly an interrogation. One wrong move from him, and she would bolt.

She glanced up when she saw him and smiled. "Not trouble I hope."

"There's always trouble in my corner," he answered easily. "The good thing is, that's what we do. We handle trouble." He deliberately emphasized his words, hoping she heard them and realized he could help her.

She cast her gaze at the water glass in front of her but didn't say anything.

"And, yes, we handle all kinds."

She shook her head. "It's not that easy."

"Trouble never is."

Then the waiter arrived with their platters of steak.

He smelled the aroma appreciatively. "This looks wonderful."

She stared at the mountain of food in front of her. "Oh, my God. I can't eat all this."

"Well, I would've agreed with you a year before, but, since then, I've met at least five women who could polish off that entire platter, down to nothing, without even trying."

She gave him a look of complete disbelief.

He nodded. "Give it a try. You might surprise yourself."

For the next ten minutes, he tackled his steak and enjoyed every bite. He made sure she kept eating. She was lean and fit, but it looked like she'd fallen on tough times. But she could eat. Once he'd given her permission to polish off the whole thing, that she didn't have to act like a debutante at a society dinner making do with a few forkfuls, he realized how long it had been since she had really eaten properly. She'd only had two sandwiches all day today.

Of course that brought up the next issue. Where the hell was she sleeping? Or, like Benji, did she not have a place to go? Then he thought about Benji, how well fed and happy he appeared to be, and realized chances were Benji had a bed to sleep in tonight. Probably a whole lot nicer than her accommodations.

Chapter 5

FROM THE FIRST bite to the last, Zoe didn't think she'd ever appreciated food quite so much. She'd grown up wealthy, had the best of everything and yet had appreciated nothing. When she hit the military, it was a whole different game. She hadn't liked the food at all. It had taken her a long time to adjust to it. But she never let anybody know.

About anything. It was the only way.

She and her father had never seen eye to eye. When she was home, she was busy doing private tutoring of some kind in her students' homes. It was a way to fill her hours, get away from her Father, and make some spending money. He hadn't wanted her to go into the military. But she'd succeeded despite him. And she had been happy there for a while.

But that had blown up too. As she swallowed the last bite of baked potato, she realized she couldn't eat any more. She set down her knife and fork and leaned back in her chair. "Oh, my God! I ate so much food."

"Good. Your body needed it."

And she realized she'd eaten twice as fast as he had. He still had vegetables and half a steak left. She winced. "Right now my mother would chastise me for my poor manners."

He raised his blue eyes and shook his head. "No judgment here. When you're hungry, the best thing you can do is eat."

She lifted her gaze to meet his. "Are you staying at Richard's house?"

He nodded. "I am, and a spare room is there for you if you want it."

She shook her head. "Better not." With that reminder she glanced around, making her once again wary.

"You can't keep running. One day you'll either get caught or run out of energy."

"Well, neither of those things will happen today." She watched as he kept eating. Eating this big meal had made her tired. One of the things about running was it was hard to rest. She was forever afraid somebody would catch up to her.

"You could tell me who you are running from." He put a bite of steak in his mouth and waited. When he could talk again, he said, "You might be surprised at the resources Levi and the company have. It doesn't matter where you go, you'll be protected."

"Maybe not."

"We've dealt with some pretty hard cases—shaken up a lot of brass in both military and law enforcement."

"Good for you. But it doesn't apply to me."

"Right." He went back to eating.

She settled into her seat a little deeper. "I just want to go to bed now," she whispered. "That's the problem with eating a big meal like that. I need a digestive nap."

"Once we get outside, the pressure will revive you."

"How are you getting to Richard's house?"

"I can either call for my guys to come get me, or I can take a cab."

She frowned at him. "Cabs are expensive."

"Life is expensive." He put the last bite of steak in his mouth and set his knife and fork on the platter. "I'm really glad you came here with me. That was excellent."

She got nervous because now he would ask for something else. One way or the other, guys always did. She knew this ahead of time, but she wasn't sure how the hell she would get out of it now. "Thank you very much for dinner," she said as she started to rise.

"Sit down," he said, his voice soft. Dangerously soft.

She slammed into her seat and glared at him. "You've got no right to keep me here."

"No, I don't, but some men just walked in the front door. And one of them looks like the guy you threw coffee on."

And she realized he wasn't angry at her. Once again he was protecting her. "Shit." She stared at him nervously. "Do you suppose the back door is open so we can make a break for it?"

He gave her a crooked smile

She was starting to recognize his moods, and she hated to say it, but was almost waiting for those different smiles. They were like a bright ray of sunshine in some very dark and gloomy days.

"I never back down from a fight as long as there's a chance I can win. In this case, how about you and I give those two morons a bad day?"

She straightened, feeling his approval and confidence like a balm to her sore, wounded soul. "As long as *I* don't get hurt. I'm not so certain about them," she admitted.

"Sure enough," he said cheerfully. "And here comes the other two."

She desperately wanted to turn around and make sure. But she knew he would not lie about something like that. "It would be nice to have your other two friends around."

"Don't worry about that. They came into the restaurant behind us."

She gasped. "Are you serious?" She was shocked at herself for not knowing. She leaned across the table and said, "I really want to look at them."

He shook his head and said, "Don't turn around. We're about to have company."

Instinctively she shifted farther over to the edge of her seat. "I'll sit here beside you." She moved her plate and coffee with one sweep.

She'd seen it happen too many times. Somebody sat in the middle of a bench seat, and then someone else sat down beside her so she couldn't get out again. Not happening today.

Suddenly shadows fell beside them. She looked up to see the guy she'd thrown coffee on and one of the others beside him. "Do you really need to be here?" she asked quietly. She picked up her coffee and held it up to him. "I don't want to lose this cup too."

His gaze hardened. "You'll get yours, bitch."

She shoved up her chin. "I might," she said in a hard voice. "I can guarantee that I'll take you out at the same time."

The other two thugs joined them. Now there were four of them again. Despite all her bravado, she could feel the nervousness slide down her soul.

Harrison, on the other hand, appeared to be completely oblivious. He leaned across the table, added some cream to his coffee and asked, "Can I help you gentlemen?"

"Yeah, now that she's got all her friends with her," said the man she'd thrown coffee on, "we would like to talk."

Zoe snorted and shook her head.

"I think you should hear what it is they want to talk about first," Harrison said.

Zoe frowned at Harrison, then said, "Absolutely."

Harrison put down his coffee cup and turned his friendly smile toward the men. "So, what's this about?"

"Zoe needs to come with us."

She stiffened. "Sorry, that's not happening. I'm currently occupied. And why do you want me anyway? You're obviously hired muscle. So, who is so interested in me that he sends four guys to collect me? That's almost an insult, you know? Surely I deserved six."

Harrison chuckled. "And now that I'm here, that's actually *very* insulting."

"Cut the crap. We have a job to do. Our orders are to pick her up. Somebody wants to talk with her."

"Absolutely," Harrison agreed. "She's willing to *talk* to somebody. But since that person didn't bother to come here, then they better arrive in the next ten minutes. Otherwise we're gone."

"He doesn't come out in public much."

"He doesn't?" Harrison asked. He deepened his tone and added, "If he wants to talk to her, he talks to her with me, and we don't appreciate the strong-arm tactics."

Zoe piped up and said, "Tell him to call me. Tell him that he can talk to me over the phone."

The men exchanged glances, not sure what to do.

"He does use a phone, I presume?"

One of the men pulled out his cell, hit a button and held it up to his ear. "Boss, she said she would talk to you over the phone." He winced at the bellow easily heard across the table.

But in a sleight-of-hand move, Zoe bounced off the

bench, snatched the phone from his hand and said, "This is Zoe. What the hell do you want with me, asshole?"

She sat down again as she registered the number on the phone. She quickly memorized it as she listened to the spluttering on the other end.

"All four men are standing here, facing me, but I'm not alone. I certainly don't expect to be strong-armed into doing what you want for nothing. If you're the asshole who shot my father and beat up my mother, I don't care how far you go or where you hide, I'll find you." She opened her mouth to blast him some more, but his voice stopped her.

He snapped, "I'm not. It wasn't me."

She froze. "Then what do you want with me?"

"I want you to know I didn't do it. You probably can do some research and see there's a history of bad blood between us. Inasmuch as I don't like your father, I respected him. He was off his rocker on some things, but at least he stood by his beliefs. Probably a few years ago, I might've done this. But I didn't. And I would never have touched your mother."

"Then why the hell don't you tell me who you are, so I can check you off my list."

"You'll figure it out soon enough."

"And my brother?" She hated to ask, but Zoe kept her voice hard, cold.

"You watch your back. Don't you step out of line too. I didn't do this, and I wouldn't touch you either. But somebody wants to take out your family. You're on somebody else's list, so make sure you keep your nose clean."

"It doesn't matter whose list I'm on if my nose is clean. I won't let anybody get to me."

There was a hard sigh on the other end of the phone, then he said, "True enough. When you see your mother again, give her my best."

And he hung up.

She ended the call, saw the name of the contact list and handed the cell off to the man. "There now, we talked. Get the hell out of my sight."

The men didn't know what to do. They milled around, uncertain for a few minutes, then left the restaurant.

She turned to face Harrison as he watched the men leave. When he settled back again, she asked, "Have they all left the building?"

He nodded. "They have, indeed." He turned to look at her. "Now what the hell was that all about?"

"The name on the contact list was Colfax. I'm sure he's been an enemy of my father's for a long time. He wanted me to know he didn't do it. And I think the reason he didn't do it is because he's sweet on my mom. There was just something about the softening in his voice when he mentioned her." She quickly relayed the extent of the conversation to Harrison.

He took notes and then pulled out his phone, making a call.

She caught the waitress's attention and asked her to bring more coffee. She didn't know if Harrison could handle any dessert after that meal they had. She was still too full but ordered a piece of cheesecake anyway. She didn't know how things would go without Harrison at her side from now on.

She vaguely remembered Colfax as the shadowy criminal figure who always escaped the law. And, if he was right, somebody was taking out her family. That meant her brother could be in trouble too. Maybe. He always escaped punishment. It was easy to see him missing out on this nightmare. Still he was her brother, rat that he was. She sent Alex a text.

Are you okay?

There was no response. Then she realized she needed to warn him.

Watch your back. Somebody is taking out the family.

No answer. She shrugged. She'd warned him. That was enough.

Harrison got off his phone and said, "Originally I thought it was more of a personal attack on your father. But, when I thought about your mother's beating as well, that changed things."

"Absolutely. Why do you think somebody's got us all on a list?"

Harrison shook his head. "No idea." When he heard her phone chime, he asked, "Have you heard from your brother? Is he safe?"

She brought up the texts and held her phone so he could see the short exchange. "He's safe. For the moment."

HARRISON WANTED TO trust she knew what she was doing. It was hard though. And went against his instincts. He'd learned a lot lately about tough, capable women. But watching Zoe, seeing what she was going through? It was not so easy to back off and let her do her own thing.

He had to wonder at her motives. Normally he was very good at reading people, but he wasn't sure at all where she stood on the issue of her brother. He leaned forward and asked, "Do you think he had anything to do with your father's attack?"

She looked at him, startled, and shook her head. "I don't think so. He was angling to get a house from our father, so I doubt he'd have taken him out. Even dead, his estate goes to Mom. We get nothing. Or so Father always told me. And Mom wasn't as quick to hand over anything to Alex. Or maybe everything's in Father's name. Who knows? Alex got what he wanted easier from Father. And Alex wanted a lot more from him."

"And if something happened to both your parents?"

"Everything's in an iron-clad trust, with monthly allowances to be doled out to each of us by a firm of grim-faced attorneys. All old. All men. Not likely to bend to Alex's whims. Again this is secondhand information from Father. I have no direct knowledge of any of this."

This time, at least, her voice had more life to it. He settled back, motioned at the table and asked, "Are you full now?"

She finished her coffee and set it next to her empty dessert plate. "I'm done. Thank you very much for dinner."

And now she was back to the polite tone of a stranger. Still figuring out her emotions, he asked for the check. When he paid the bill, he said, "Come on. Let's go."

They walked through the restaurant and out the front door. When they stood on the steps, she asked, "Where are we going?"

He turned to study her. "Where do you want to go? I offered you a place at Richard's house. Do you have better lodgings? Do you have safer lodgings?"

"Colfax only wanted to get a hold of me to let me know he had nothing to do with the attacks on my parents."

"And those four thugs were his men, right?"

She nodded. "Yes."

"So, is it safe to go home now that you know they won't be after you anymore?"

She stiffened and glared at him. "No, I won't go home. Ever."

And she turned to the right and stormed off down the sidewalk. He watched her for a long moment, wondering if she would disappear from his sight. Right now, in her current mental state, he could say the wrong thing, and she would fire off like a bullet.

"That's your MO, right? Something happens, and you run," he called behind her.

She spun around, crying out, "That's not fair. You don't know me enough to make that assessment."

"Something happens in the army, you run. Something happens at home, same thing. I say the wrong thing, you run."

She shook her head. "I didn't run from the army. I tried so damn hard to change things. To make her death matter. At home, there's no home to return to. Remember? My mother is in the hospital. My father is dying. What would I possibly return home for? And as for you, I've been on the verge of walking away since I first met you." She gave him the sweetest fake smile she could manage and turned on her heels, heading off again in the direction she had been walking.

Instead of being angry, he had to admit seeing that porcupine again was fun. He started to laugh, falling in step behind her, though she was quite a way ahead of him. But now that he was laughing at her, he could see her hands clenching into fists as her steps moved faster. Of course, that wouldn't work, as he could easily keep up.

As he rounded the corner and strode up the side street,

she stopped and said, "You don't have to look after me anymore. I'm perfectly capable of taking care of myself."

"Sure you are. Maybe I need to look after the rest of the world. Maybe you're a danger to them." He hadn't meant the words in any way, except that nothing made sense yet, and he needed her to talk to him. To trust him. And he wanted her to let something slip about her past. In his mind, he was already thinking about calling Levi to get the details about Zoe and her friend who had died, but Harrison needed a few minutes alone for that.

She shot him an uncertain look and said, "I've never hurt anybody who didn't deserve it."

He nodded. "I can't say the same. A lot of people's definition of what *deserve* means is different from ours. Just because we have somebody in our lives, doesn't mean we have the right to turn around and hurt them."

"I've never hurt anybody like that," she said softly but took off down the sidewalk again.

He didn't change the pace of his stride, but when she stopped once more, he stood in front of her. "And right now, I'd like to know that you have a place to sleep tonight. A safe one where you won't get into more trouble."

"What kind of trouble?"

"Your father's been shot. Your mother's been beaten. How do you know the person who did that isn't after you?"

She turned her head to stare off in the distance at some point of interest beyond his shoulder. He watched her features twist as she concentrated. "He was shot on the front doorstep. The chances are he opened the door to the gunman. I don't know how my mom got involved. She'd have done a lot to avoid that." She gave him a shuttered look and said, "My father is abusive. He hits her—sometimes badly."

Inside Harrison something settled, it was hard, deep, and ugly. "So he's a wife-beater?" He kept his voice low. He was busy, sending a text to Levi. Lots of interesting tidbits here.

She nodded. "Yes, always has been. He tried to beat us when we were little. Mom managed to stop Alex from being abused, but not me and because she never could stop Father from beating her, they escalated. I tried to step in, tried to stop him, but she would always tell me to leave him alone. That he needed the outlet."

"He could have gone to a gym and used an actual punching bag."

She stared at that same place in the distance. "We told her that. Many times." She shook her head. "It never made any difference."

He'd seen too many similar cases to go over the same hollow excuses as to why women stayed when they were beaten. Often they stayed out of guilt, or twisted love. But he suspected that by taking the beatings, she was protecting her kids.

"Any time he raised a hand to us, she'd step in and take the blow."

He hooked his arm through hers, gently clasping her hand. "So you don't think he beat her up before he was injured? Or maybe he was shot to stop him from hurting her?"

She shook her head. "I don't know. I heard about the beating on the news, but I doubt anyone was there at the time. Father didn't like anyone to know what he was doing."

"Where was your brother during all this?"

"Who knows? He lives at home part time but has another place. We're not close." She gave a half snort. "Meaning, I have nothing to do with him. Alex certainly is mean and petty but isn't very aggressive. He's more a pretty playboy. He was home that evening as he was at dinner with us, but I left. Maybe he did too." She shrugged. "If he did try to kill our father, he's smart enough to have an alibi."

"And you?"

She shot him that same shuttered look. "I live alone. Since I left the military, I've been staying in a cheap furnished apartment until I sort out my life. I don't have many friends, and, since this happened, I've been living on the streets. That means, no alibi. I was extremely resentful of my father for always beating my mother, and I was angry her for staying, and according to the police, that's likely lots of motive. I also have a big chip on my shoulder right now. And I hate authority. And if I thought I could cut off the head of the snake at its source—and chop off law enforcement and the military's evils all at the same time—I would do it."

"Interesting that you put the two of those together," he said. "And just because there might be a bad apple or a bushel within the thousands of people who work in both those areas, that doesn't mean that either system is *completely* wrong or that the people therein are *all* bad."

Chapter 6

SHE WANTED TO tell Harrison everything. But she didn't know this man. She didn't dare trust him. She hated strangers. And superiors. And coworkers. She glared at the darkening evening around her. Goddammit. How had her life come to this?

"Are you sure you don't want a nice bed for the night? And a shower?"

"Do I stink?"

His eyebrows rose. "No. But that's no reason not to accept an offer of help, is it?"

Disgruntled, she shook her head. "Fine. But I don't want to bring more trouble to Richard. How about we go someplace completely different?"

"Why?" He grabbed her by the arm and pulled her around so she was facing him. "Aside from your family being targeted, do you bring a particular danger with you wherever you go? Are you running from something? Why would going to Richard's put him in harm's way?"

"No particular reason, except, as you pointed out, somebody could be wiping out my family."

He nodded. "But Richard's place has round-the-clock security. And somebody would have to know you were there. If that's the case, then somebody already knows where you are now."

She shook her head. "Look, you don't have to stick with me. I get this is a job. But it's really got nothing to do with me. I didn't shoot my father, and I didn't beat up my mother. I want you to take all that energy and misguided concern and find out who really did." She watched him glare at her and cross his arms over his chest. She sighed. "You really do have a hero complex, don't you?" At that she could almost see him snapping his eyebrows together in a fit of temper. It was her turn to raise her brows. "So, you don't like that term. Whatever. The thing is, I'm fine. And I'll stay fine. And I don't want to bring any trouble to Richard. Just in case."

"Okay, then where do we stay?"

She shrugged. "There is a homeless center around here. I'm sure I can grab a bed for the night."

He brought up his watch. "It's almost eleven. Not only will it be closed but the beds might be full."

He was right. "I'll find a park bench then." Although she didn't feel safe enough to actually sleep in the open like that. If only she could make peace with herself and the miserable events that had dominated her for the last two years, and then all these considerations would cease.

He shook his head. "No way I'll sleep on a park bench."

"Maybe they can bring out a cot at the hospital, and I can stay with my mom overnight. She's under guard, so I'd be safe too. That's perfect." She pulled out her phone and the card Richard had given her. "Richard," she said when he answered the phone. "Any chance I could have a cot brought to my mom's room, and I could stay there with her tonight?"

"I'm not sure that's best for her right now. She's been surfacing and going under, but she's distraught. If she wakes up to find you there, I don't know what kind of reaction it will bring up. If I thought it would make her happy, that would be perfect, and I'd be all for it. But because I don't know, I'm not sure that's the best way forward."

"But I can come visit, right?"

"You can visit her in the morning. She is settled for the night," he said cautiously. "What's this all about?"

"I was looking at my options for the night."

"Your best option is to go to my house. But I'm sure Harrison has already told you that."

"Yes, he has, but I don't want to bring any trouble to your doorstep. You're already helping my mother. What if anything happened to you? That won't be very good either," she said in a half-joking manner.

"Right. So trouble is dogging your heels. Well, I have good security at home, and, if needed, I can bring in a few more men."

"There's got to be another answer."

"There is," Harrison said in a loud, hard voice. "I'll grab a hotel for the two of us."

"Like hell you will."

"Richard, what do you think?"

"I think you are both being foolish. You should go to my place. I have a ton of guest rooms."

Harrison glared at her. "Two choices. Hotel—with me sharing the same room—or Richard's, where you get your own."

She was so mad she stomped her foot on the cement. And then she gave a barely withheld scream of fury. When she realized Richard was laughing, she snapped, "Fine. But it's not my fault if someone follows us there."

"I hope he does," Harrison growled. "Maybe this will come to a head. By the time I get him tied up in a chair and get answers from the asshole, we'll know exactly what the hell's going on."

Richard said, "How long will it take you to get here? I'm having a nightcap, so hurry up."

"We still don't have a way to get there," Zoe said. "It'll be almost impossible to call a cab from here."

"There are other means." Harrison raised his hand in the air and gave a wave.

What the hell was he doing?

The Jeep she'd been in earlier drove up behind them. He motioned to the front seat and asked, "How about this? Would you accept a ride again?"

Her jaw dropped as she recognized the same two men. "You're telling me that they've been following us the whole time?" She was put out she hadn't even noticed. She blamed Harrison for that. She hopped in the front seat, glanced at the almost Icelandic-looking man driving and said, "Thank you for the ride. I don't think I introduced myself earlier. I'm Zoe."

The big man gave her a gentle smile and said, "No problem. I'm Saul."

The darker guy in the back said, "And I'm Dakota."

Harrison hopped into the back seat and said, "Richard's place, please, guys. After that, you're off duty."

"Our first job as babysitter has been pretty easy," Saul said with a grin.

Then came a hard ping on the side of the Jeep.

Saul's foot hit the pedal, and the Jeep raced forward.

Zoe spun around and stared at Harrison. "Was that a gunshot?"

He placed his big hand on the back of her head and forced her down. "Stay low."

The men checked their surroundings. Saul did a series of quick zigzags and turns. She studied the street signs as she lay prone on the seat to realize they'd returned to where they'd been shot at a few minutes earlier.

Saul drove slowly so the guys could see if anyone followed them.

As far as she was concerned, returning to the scene of the crime set them up to be a target twice. "What? Are you trying to get shot at again?"

The street was empty. Harrison let her sit up again. Saul took off, taking a very confusing route through the city, back and around, lots of left turns, right turns, and heading toward one of the wealthier districts in San Diego. When he pulled up outside a secure gated area and identified himself, the gates opened, and they drove through. She heard Harrison on the phone, talking to Richard.

"We're in the compound. Lock down security. We were shot at."

The lights outside amped up, and she had no idea what else went on. But she imagined security for this place was rather solid. The big mansion was ahead of her with a small house off to the side. "Why would one person live in something so big?"

"He used to live here with his daughter, but she now lives with Levi in Texas," Harrison said.

"She's the other part of Legendary Security." That explained a few things.

Harrison exited the Jeep, quickly opened her door and ushered her into the house. There were no incidents getting inside. Saul and Dakota came in also, and Harrison asked them, "Are you heading home, or do you want to stay here for the night?"

Saul nodded. "Like hell we're leaving at this point."

"Good," Richard said, joining them. "Now I don't have to hire more men. My daughter just hired them for me instead." Richard beamed at the group of four, standing at the front door. "Also helpful that I have lots of room here. You want to be on the same floor upstairs?" He turned to Harrison. "I trust I can leave room assignments to your choosing?"

Harrison nodded. "She'll be in the room next to me, and I'll have one of the guys on the other side." He faced Richard. "What about you?"

"I'll be in bed in about ten minutes, and I don't plan to leave my room until tomorrow morning." He gave a tired smile to the group. "As much as I like company, it's been quite a long and difficult day. Tomorrow will not be much better. I have several very difficult surgeries. If you need food, the kitchen is to the left. If you need booze, the bar is right ahead. I trust you can help yourselves without needing a host." As he headed upstairs, he added, "Breakfast is at seven." At that, he disappeared.

"He really does have a lot of space, doesn't he?" Zoe said. "My father's house is big, but it's not like this."

"He's been threatening to sell it for a long time," Harrison said.

"And then what? What about his hospital?"

"If he didn't have that, I think he'd moved closer to Ice, but maybe not for a while yet."

The four of them moved upstairs. Harrison took a left when they got to the top. He quickly motioned Dakota and Saul to their rooms, then opened the door to his and said, "This is mine, and you're in the adjoining room."

"Adjoining room?" She glared at him suspiciously.

"Does it have a connecting door?"

"Yes, they have a connecting door," he said drily. "I promise I won't come in and try to seduce you in the night."

Saul and Dakota held back their chuckles.

Zoe shot them a glare.

Harrison opened the door to her room and walked inside the massive suite. He pointed to the door to the right, centered in a wall. "That leads to my room. You can lock it if you want. However, for the sake of security, it would be nice if you didn't. I can pick that lock in about ten seconds flat, but, if you have an intruder, that ten seconds is a couple bullets' worth of time."

She stood inside the entranceway, her arms crossed over her chest, her foot tapping impatiently on the floor.

"What? The accommodations not to your liking?"

"The accommodations are superb, as you well know. But you can leave any time."

He laughed and walked past her, gently brushing a hand across the top of her head. He stopped and said, "Oh, look at that. The porcupine quills don't stand straight up when you're touched."

And he walked out, still laughing. She slammed the door shut behind him. She turned to face the room, which was wonderful. If only she could get a shower and manage a good night's sleep, then get the hell out of here before anybody woke, that would really be ideal.

HE REALLY SHOULDN'T tease her, but it was damn hard not to. Yet the fulminating look she had sent his way had only heightened his enjoyment. And she needed to get rid of that chip on her shoulder. If he kept knocking it off, maybe it would stay that way. He walked into his room and closed the door. He really could use a shower and bed himself. But he had to update Levi.

He opened his laptop and quickly wrote a detailed email. After he sent it off, he stripped and took a shower. Ten minutes later, as he got in bed, he could barely see a slice of light under her door. He frowned. Was she having trouble sleeping? Was she worrying about something? It'd been a good half hour since he had left her.

He sighed. He'd better check. At the connecting door he gently turned the knob. The door opened under his hand. Good. He stuck his head through the doorway. Every light was on, but she was sound asleep in bed. He frowned, gently closed the door and returned to his own bed. Was she terrified of the dark? She didn't have just one light on; she had the lamp on by the easy chair and the other two as well as the overhead light. *Interesting.*

He couldn't imagine what her childhood had been like. If her father beat her mother, that would be tough enough. To fail to convince your mother to leave would've added to Zoe's frustration. And yet it was the same old story all over the world. People got into these difficult relationships, and it was hard to find a way out.

He turned off his light and settled in under the covers. But his mind wouldn't quit churning.

He knew Saul was worried about the Jeep and had done a quick search of the vehicle before coming up the front steps. But he never said anything. So far, Harrison had been quite impressed with both Saul and Dakota. They had been buddies in the military, serving in the same SEAL unit, and both had walked away over the same issue. Harrison hadn't pushed, hadn't asked what that was. But sometimes the men were put in difficult situations where their own personal honor came up against their orders.

He knew Flynn had walked away for that reason. Well, maybe Flynn had a little help leaving, as he had disobeyed a direct order. But with Dakota and Saul, it'd been their choice. When you couldn't trust the men behind you, and didn't believe in those men, what you were doing no longer made sense. Maybe one day, when they were part of the unit and felt comfortable enough, they'd open up about what had happened. Every one of these men in Levi's unit had been there, done that. They'd all been forced to face issues that normally they wouldn't have to. But being asked to do something that was wrong was,…well, wrong. When you were ordered to do it, disobeying an order came with severe penalties. Sometimes the definition of what was right changed.

He drifted off to sleep only to sit up wide awake at an odd sound. He checked his watch. It was 1:30 a.m. He got out of bed and walked to the connecting door, putting his ear against it. He couldn't hear anything else. But what he'd heard had been enough to wake him. He opened the door and stuck his head around the edge. The room was empty except for her. She tossed and turned in the bed. Whimpering. He watched her for a long moment, wondering if he should wake her. She whimpered once more and then seemed to ease into asleep again.

Everyone had nightmares. But in her case, they were likely to be much worse than most. He understood. He never had any PTSD problems himself, but he knew lots of men who did. And it was awful. Sometimes the guys woke up, not understanding what world they were in, and their reactions were instantaneous, instinctual. And, all too often, lethal.

But she had quieted, settled. He slipped out again and returned to his bed. He punched his pillow, rolled over and fell asleep.

Several hours later he rolled on his back to see the doorknob turn on the connecting door. He shifted in bed and pretended to sleep. Under his lashes, he watched as the door opened. All the lights were still on in her room, sending a halo of light through his. She poked her head in, and then, as if seeing him, she relaxed.

"Can't sleep?"

She shifted in surprise. "I didn't mean to wake you."

"Not a problem." He sat up, careful to not make any fast movements, in case it caused her to bolt. "Did you get any sleep?"

"I did, but I woke up from a nightmare," she confessed. "It's too early to leave yet," she said. "I thought I heard someone downstairs. Wondered if maybe you guys were up already."

He glanced at his watch and said, "It's only five. Can you sleep some more?"

She shook her head. "No, I'm done for the night."

"I guess I am too. Are you ready for breakfast? It's not for two hours yet."

"A walk if you're up for it," she said in a light challenge. "You mentioned a good run. You okay with that? Because I could really use a workout."

"Are you dressed for it?"

"I only have these clothes with me." She shrugged. "But it's not like I can't run in what I'm wearing. I have my sneakers on."

"Give me five."

She gave him a faint smile. "Hurry up." She closed the

door with a *click*.

He shook his head, quickly checked through his bag for his shorts, threw on a muscle shirt, grabbed his running shoes and walked out into the hallway. She was there waiting for him. "Let's hope Richard or his staff are up so we can leave the compound without setting off his security system."

She froze on the stairs. "I didn't think about that."

He led the way to the kitchen. And, sure enough, there was Foster, making a pot of coffee.

He turned in surprise and said, "Aren't you two up early."

"We're going for a run. Can you shut off security so we can get out?"

Foster nodded. "I'll give you three minutes to get to the front door, and then I'll shut it down. You've got four minutes to cross the lawn and exit the gate, and then it'll turn back on again. Call me when you need to come back in."

And that was what they did. By the time they made it through the gate and hit the main road, she was flat-out running. This wasn't a jog. She had places to go, things to do, and she would get them all done right now apparently.

"This is the pace you always jog at?"

She shook her head. "No. But the nightmare has me all wired up. I feel the need to keep running away." She picked up her speed. Again.

All he could do was attempt to stay with her.

Chapter 7

IT HAD BEEN a tough night for her. Nightmares, screams, endless running in the dark. She'd woken several times, struggling through the sheets in a panic to find herself in a room she didn't recognize and in a space she didn't know.

Scary stuff.

When she'd woken the last time, she knew she had to do something to shed the tension. Instead of easing it through a good night's sleep, she found it had twisted her gut and ripped at her soul.

Running was the only answer, even if it didn't make sense that doing so physically would help her stop in her nightmares.

She couldn't afford to stand still in life right now because it seemed everyone and everything was after her—and yet she had no proof anyone was. She knew she'd made trouble for a group of military assholes, and if they were after her… She'd heard her father had been shot and her mother badly beaten. She figured whoever did that would now either pin those actions on her or would take her out next.

Of course the cops were interested in her whereabouts. How could they not be? She'd been at her parents' house earlier the night her father had been shot. She'd been checking the news on her phone ever since and saw the media coverage. Nothing made any sense, and because of that, she ran…to get away from all the unknowns she couldn't deal with.

And because she worried evidence had been planted to make her look guilty as hell.

It didn't take long for the running to provide the magic she looked for. Forgetfulness. As her muscles leaned out and stretched, she pumped forward at a rate she could barely control. Need drove her on. She could feel the tension ease off her back, along with the sweat. She ran and ran and ran.

She glanced beside her to see Harrison holding his pace easily at her side. Just from the length of his stride alone, he could keep up with her. She envied him. He seemed to have the endurance to go another 10K. Whereas, now that they headed toward the 15K mark—according to her watch—she was wearing down.

She glanced around and asked, "Time to head back?"

"Sounds good. You up for the full distance back or a shortcut?"

She considered her energy stores and said, "Shortcut."

He pointed and said, "Let's head this way. We can take this path and shave off several miles."

She nodded and followed his lead this time. Maybe that was better. She had him set the pace, and he maintained it—slow, steady, eating at the miles with his long stride. She'd do her damnedest to keep up.

Forty minutes later they arrived at the front gates again. He slowed and continued jogging on the spot. He called Foster to say they were here. She jogged in place, then slowed to a walk and finally stretched and shook out her limbs. Not only had that been more miles than she had expected, but she hadn't done a run like that in a long time. She would be sore tomorrow. Now if she could find a hot tub or a swimming pool inside, that would help.

As they walked through the gate and up to the house, Harrison said, "Thank you. That was a great run." He reached his arms above his head and did several arms stretches.

"You're right. It was good." She chuckled. "I usually find it to be a great way to get rid of my demons."

He headed for the door and opened it for her. "And running keeps you in shape, so if the demons in your world do rise, you're fit enough to get away."

She nodded. "I hope Richard has a large hot water tank because I may stand under the showerhead for a full hour."

"Go ahead. Breakfast is at seven, so you've got like ten minutes." He chuckled at her look. "And I'd rather eat than stand under a hot shower for too long. I can get dressed and be down there on time, but you're a woman so …"

She shot him a sideways glance. "Race you to it."

"Are you competitive in everything you do?"

She shook her head. "No, but I do find it's a great way to get things done and done fast."

"You're on." He raced up the stairs three at a time.

His long legs ate up the distance. She had no hope of catching up, but she ran after him anyway. "Hey, that's cheating."

"You wanted a challenge." He disappeared into his room.

She bolted inside hers, stripped off her clothes and got under the hot water.

She shampooed her hair and decided she'd rather lose her race with Harrison to make sure she was nice and truly clean. She turned off the water and stepped outside the shower to dry off. Wrapped in a towel, she walked into her room, wondering what the hell her clothing options were now. She wasn't about to wear her sweaty clothes after just getting clean.

There was a knock at the door. Harrison said, "Hey, I beat you."

She walked to the door, still wrapped in her towel, and peered around it. "Yeah, that's a hell of a way to beat me," she said. "I don't have a thing to wear."

He leered at her lasciviously, a comical look in his eyes. "You don't think it was my plan the whole time?" He held out a stack of clothes.

She rolled her eyes and looked at the stuff in his hands. "Where did you get those? And women's clothes at that?"

"Foster brought them from Ice's old room."

"Do we have the same body type?" she asked.

He held up leggings and a T-shirt. "I figured even if they were too long, they'd still work. And the legs can always be rolled up if they drag the ground." He handed the clothes to her. "You got three minutes to make it for breakfast."

She took the clothes, surprised to find a couple options in underwear to choose from, and quickly dressed. She realized he was right. Given his earlier description of Ice as an Amazon warrior, the leggings were probably three-quarter-calf length for her, but for Zoe, they went right to her ankles. And that was fine. Throwing on the T-shirt, she flicked a brush through her hair and braided it. As she walked into the kitchen, she twisted the ends together so it would stay for a while.

Foster smiled at her. "Good morning." He walked to a cabinet, pulled out a drawer and came up with a rubber band. "Not ideal."

She laughed. "No, but it's not far off." She tied off the

bottom of her braid. She looked around. "Anything I can do?"

He shook his head. "Go take a seat."

Doorways went off in all directions from the kitchen. She leaned closer and said, "I would if I knew which direction to go."

He winked and walked her through a door to the right into a huge dining room.

She was the last one to arrive. She glared at Harrison.

Harrison chuckled.

"Coffee's over there." Foster pointed to the sideboard where a complete coffee service awaited.

"I told you that women always take much longer."

"I did have a slight handicap, as you know, with no clothes to wear."

"I gave you a solution to that."

"Yeah, sure enough. *After* you were fully dressed."

She poured her coffee and sat next to Richard. "Good morning."

He studied her carefully.

She knew the doctor in him couldn't resist assessing her health and mental state. She gave him a bright smile and said, "The run this morning helped a lot."

Instead of smiling back, he frowned. "Did you not sleep?"

She nodded. "I did, just not the greatest."

"Oh, dear, I should've thought of that. I do have something to help, if you need it tonight."

She opened her mouth and started to shake her head but felt the kick to her leg. She frowned at Harrison to see him sending her a way-too-innocent-looking smile. She didn't know what he was up to, but she remained silent, glaring in his direction.

Then Foster came in with a trolley, loaded with several big serving dishes with silver lids.

She smiled. When he removed the lids, the aroma wafted through the room. She lifted her nose appreciatively. "It smells lovely, Foster."

He unloaded platters of bacon and sausages. When he uncovered a serving tray of pancakes, she almost crowed in delight. He followed that up with a large platter of scrambled eggs. "I'll be back in a few minutes with toast."

Everyone passed around the serving trays until they had helped themselves.

She had no compunction about eating now. She grabbed several flapjacks, loading up on bacon and sausages. By the time the eggs arrived, she added them to her plate. She picked up her fork and knife. The trouble was, she didn't want to eat fast; she wanted to enjoy this meal. She'd been a little short on food rations lately. And some food just required savoring.

Foster came back, took a seat with them, and she felt better. In her father's house, the staff were not welcome at the family table. She was glad that wasn't the case here.

When she finished, Zoe gently pushed away her plate, almost feeling well enough to face the world. Now back to the question she'd been biting her tongue over. "Richard, how's my mom?"

He nodded his head regally and said, "She's doing better. She had a good night. But she's still sleeping deep. So when she wakes, she's confused and not very cognizant."

"May I see her this morning?"

He nodded. "Absolutely. We can go after breakfast if you'd like."

She nodded, picked up her cup and refilled her coffee. She brought the pot over to the table and proceeded to fill the empty cups. After returning the pot, she sat again.

Richard looked at her. "What are your plans for the day, my dear?"

She shook her head. "I'm not sure yet. See my mom, check on my father's condition. Find out who shot at us last night."

Richard gasped. "You were really shot at?"

She nodded. "I imagine Saul checked the Jeep for damage."

Saul's face hardened. "It hit us. Thankfully in a spot that didn't really matter—the metal of the tire rack."

She raised her eyebrow. "Nice. Of all the places they could hit, that's the best one."

He nodded. "I wouldn't take kindly to having my baby splattered with gunfire."

"Any news yet?" asked Richard.

"Not for the moment," Harrison said. "I'm about to call Levi. I gave him an update last night, but he's waiting for us this morning."

"Us?" Zoe asked.

He nodded. "His text message said he wanted to speak with you too."

She dropped her elbows on the table and glared at him. "You know there's no *us* involved, right? I was doing fine until you showed up and dragged me all over the place. I don't know Levi, and, no insult to Richard, I don't know his daughter either." She shot an apologetic look toward Richard.

He inclined his head and said, "I hope you do get a chance to meet her. She's very special."

"From what I've heard, they both are," Zoe said. "I'm just not sure I want anything to do with anybody at this time."

Saul stared at her and asked, "Why did you leave the military?"

She turned a flat stare his way. "My time was up."

He raised an eyebrow. "And yet you went from being the best of the best, top of the class, to suddenly having trouble with authority and major anger issues."

Inside her heart sank. She wanted to say it was none of their business. But she knew she would have to answer their questions eventually. No matter how she tried, her experience with the military would haunt her forever. "Life happens. Our perspectives change. We view things in a different way. I lost all respect for the military. I couldn't follow their rules anymore. And the orders from superiors became an insult. I had to get out."

The men exchanged glances.

She added, "I don't care if you believe me or not."

"We believe you," Harrison said. "We've all bucked up against orders, personnel we didn't like, pencil pushers who ran things but didn't know what it was like outside in the real world." He shrugged. "Not one of us here doesn't understand that."

She settled back.

"I guess what I'm asking," Saul said, "or rather should come right out and ask is, whether what happened to you back then has anything to do with what's happening to you now?"

She frowned. "I don't think so." Of course she'd considered the same thing.

The last thing she wanted was to revisit that nightmare.

Yet it wouldn't let her go. She really didn't want to explain it to these men. If it did have something to do with these current events, then she was in trouble. There would be no way to avoid a full-on discussion. Harrison would insist she tell him everything.

Something she didn't want to do.

WHAT WOULD IT take to make her share what happened in the military? Harrison didn't know if it was connected to the recent attacks on her father and mother, but it was sure as hell connected to who she was today. Because that woman who entered the military, maybe out of defiance, maybe out of eagerness, had come out bitter and angry. He knew the pathway for women in the military was very different than for men. He'd heard lots of stories, knew lots of women who had come and gone. Some had fit the mold and done beautifully; others couldn't take the male-dominated world that barely respected women in many ways, and had left. He could easily see something like that being Zoe's problem. Yet he was afraid it was more than that.

Sexual harassment abounded in the military. He hoped it wasn't anything as nasty as that. But no doubt she was not the same person who'd gone in. And then there was the issue of her dead friend.

As he reflected on his life in the military, he realized he had been the one who had the problem with relationships. He'd had a fiancée he'd planned to marry when he went to training. She had been very accepting. He had found out afterward she'd been having an affair the whole time. It had made him bitter. Especially as he'd found her in bed with her lover—his brother—to add to the pain. He'd learned to control his temper, to find patience, tolerance and acceptance.

Maybe Zoe had learned a lot too. But she'd also learned something else. Distrust. And that was a bad thing as it would be hard for him to get close to her when she was so angry. He had watched her run in a mad pique this morning, eating up the miles. Making him run twice as hard to keep up with her. She ran to rid herself of the demons bedeviling her—not for the joy of experiencing the way her body felt, the healthy power of her muscles working.

He understood. He'd had many a similar workout.

His phone buzzed, and he saw Levi's name. Knew Levi had more on Zoe's military file. Harrison stood and excused himself from the table. "I should check on some paperwork Levi sent. I'll be about ten to fifteen minutes. When I'm done, we should give him a call and then head to the hospital so you can see your mom."

She nodded, her gaze hooded, her thoughts far away.

He waited for a moment to see if she had really connected with what he said.

She waved her hand. "Go. I'll have another cup of coffee, and then, if I must talk to Levi, I will. I do want to go see Mom soon though."

He nodded and walked to his room, grabbing his laptop and quickly checking the email Levi had sent. The files were restricted. In other words, somebody high up had seen the value of an investigation into Zoe and had supplied information. He sat back and read.

And what he found pissed him off.

Tamara Vettering. She'd been gang-raped one morning. Zoe had found her and had called for medical help, and Tamara had survived physically, but emotionally she been extremely traumatized.

But the men all appeared—somehow—to have alibis. Her story was dismissed with the doctor saying her injuries appeared to be self-inflicted. Harrison raised his gaze to stare at the far wall.

"How did one *self-inflict* rape wounds? Impaling herself with what? And why?"

Tamara wanted to leave the military before finishing out her years. She'd fought strenuously to have the men court-martialed. But apparently no semen had been found; they had no DNA evidence. She'd been in the showers. Everything washed away. No fingerprints. No witnesses as they deemed Tamara not credible. And the entire incident had been pushed aside.

He reached up and rubbed his face. "If it actually happened, and Zoe had known it for sure or had truly believed her friend, then nothing the military said would have been good enough for her. She'd want justice."

He returned to his reading and then winced. Tamara, unable to handle the mockery, the complete change in atmosphere around her afterward, committed suicide. In the same showers where she'd been raped. And again Zoe found her friend.

Harrison leaned back and closed his eyes. "Shit."

Of course she was angry. Of course she was hurting. Of course she wanted justice but felt she wasn't likely to get it. And, even if she did, it was way too late.

Unfortunately, accusations of sexual assault, abuse, and harassment ran rampant throughout the military. He understood it was a big problem. But not enough was done. They had to protect those women who stepped up to serve their country.

"That's why Zoe walked."

He quickly ran through the rest of the paperwork, realizing Zoe hadn't given up. She'd fought to have Tamara's case reopened and to have the men brought to trial. Justice for her friend. No mention was made of the names of the men involved. *Of course not. It would've sullied their military records.*

But Tamara had been mocked by the others in her world. Another reason so many rape victims never spoke up. When she committed suicide, Tamara drifted into the level of a statistic: *yet another woman who couldn't handle a man's world.*

Harrison sat for a long moment. Tamara might not have been the best type of person for the military. She might have needed professional help. She certainly needed help if this was self-inflicted. And, if she'd been raped, she needed all the support that everybody had to give her. But instead she'd been forced to take what had been dished out. And take and take. Until nothing was left, and she ended up taking her life.

He got up from his laptop, anger coursing through him. He stared at his closed fists and realized that, no matter how or why it happened, he hated injustice.

He generally liked and respected most military personnel. Right now, he wasn't feeling very cordial to any of them. That he was no longer part of that huge machine was probably a good thing. As he had loosened up, relaxed and joined Levi's group, it had become that much harder to stick himself back into the mold of being a good SEAL. He was a better man now that he was out. He also came with a perspective that was a little easier to handle. There was just so much more to the world than the military allowed. He loved what he was doing now.

He had served his country. But with Legendary Security, he didn't have to deal with people who gave orders when some were ones Harrison could not admire.

He walked out the bedroom door and headed downstairs. His phone buzzed again, and it was Levi. Harrison sent a text, saying he was locating Zoe for the conference call. He walked into the kitchen. No sign of her. He glanced around in the dining room, but it was empty.

Foster said, "She headed up to her room to collect her clothes."

Harrison nodded. "Okay, I'll go check." He hoped that was all she was up to. Because if she was off and running again, that wasn't good news.

At her door, he stopped and knocked. No answer came from the inside. Hating his suspicions, he pushed open the door and stepped in. The bedroom was empty, but her clothes were still here. And the bathroom door was closed. "Zoe? Are you there? We're ready to call Levi."

Her response from the bathroom reassured him. "Be there in five."

He didn't want to stay in the hall, so he stood in the doorway and waited for her to come out.

Chapter 8

ZOE PUT AWAY her washcloths and towels and cleaned up the bathroom. She didn't want to appear like a poor guest. Her mama had taught her better than that. With a last glance around, her dirty clothes in her bag, she stepped into the main suite.

Harrison leaned against the entryway to her room, his arms crossed over his chest. He glanced at her bag and said, "If you want to pick up the rest of your luggage, you can do laundry here."

She twisted her lips. "I've no idea what I'll be doing, where I'll be going."

"You should do something with your life."

"Not until I get a few things settled."

He shifted away from the door and walked toward the stairs. "You also should pick something in life that you can fight for. But fight smart." He stared straight ahead as he spoke.

She studied his profile. What was going on behind that flat gaze? Then she got it. "Did you read my file?"

He raised an eyebrow but didn't lie. "Of course I did. And your brother, mother and father's."

She hunched her shoulders. "Of course you would have."

"Your father is dying. Your mother's been badly beaten.

In addition, your father is a senator, in a prominent position. You really think everyone is *not* trying to find out what happened and catch the person responsible?"

"You didn't have to dig into my background. Pry through the details of my private life."

"Would you have told me?"

At that hardened tone, she winced. "It's personal and private."

"There's nothing personal or private about it now. You survived against all kinds of hell, and that's a matter of record. Everyone knows you are angry. That you want justice for your friend."

"It didn't do one damn bit of good," she said bitterly.

"Tell me, how can you be so sure she was raped?"

She winced, his words confirming her worst fears. "Because I knew her. I knew the assholes too."

"And yet had no way to prove it."

She shook her head. "Only that they'd done it before."

He stopped and turned to stare at her. "Are you sure?"

"We met with several other women to get them to join together and have a lawyer represent them all in a class action lawsuit. But in the military, it's not that easy. The women were terrified." She shook her head. "I could hardly blame them. What they'd gone through was already traumatic enough. But it had to end somewhere. Unfortunately, Tamara chose her end, and I wasn't fast enough to stop her."

"And you can't let it go?" Harrison sent her a sidelong glance. "Are you still fighting her fight? Are you hunting them?"

She faltered. When she regained control, she asked, "Hunting who?" From the look he gave her, she understood just how much he knew her already. She raised her hands in the air. "Not really. I want to make them pay, but legally. Yet I can't find the way to do it, which is why I'm so angry—and frustrated. I can't stand to let those assholes get away with it."

Harrison nodded. "What are their names?" He pulled out his phone.

She contemplated that for a long moment. Could he do anything to help? "Paul Canley, Jeff Jorgensen, Lawrence Hitchcock, Randy Maguire, and Lee Wilson."

He typed in the names as she said each one and sent them to Levi.

"Do you really think Levi gives a shit?"

Harrison gave her a hard glance. "Levi gives a shit about a lot of things, and there are a couple that *none* of us tolerate, and rape is one of them. Wife-beating is another." He speared her with an intense glare. "We will do our best to make sure these men are held accountable for what has been done."

She snorted. "You think I haven't heard that from three dozen military men over the last two years?" She shook her head. "None of them meant it."

"Well, that's them. Not us. And maybe we can make a difference."

She broke out laughing but with a hard edge to it.

"Shit." He grabbed her arm and pulled her toward him. "Do any of these men have anything to do with the attacks on your father and mother?"

"I wish I knew," she cried out. "I really want those assholes to go down. And I want them to pay for all they've done."

"They ever attack you?"

She shook her head. "One of them tried. I broke two of

his fingers."

"Good for you."

She shook her head. "I should have broken his boner."

"Ouch."

"It's what he deserved."

Harrison shrugged. "Maybe, but as a male, I can't say I like the sound of that." They walked through the living room.

"Where the hell are we going?"

"Richard's office."

"Why?"

"Soundproofed and debugged. It has security to stop anybody from hacking in and hearing our conversations."

"Okay, the superspy stuff. It's kind of freaky for a doctor. Why the hell does he have any of this?"

"Because he talks with Ice all the time. Father and daughter don't want to watch every word they say to each other." He shrugged. "I set it up for him. It's still very convenient for us when we visit."

"I'll say."

At the office, she found Dakota and Saul waiting. She nodded at them. "Is this a conference call?"

Levi's voice filled the room. "Zoe, Ice is on the phone here with me and a few more of our men. What exactly did you see that night you saw your father? And share anything you may have heard."

She glared at the speakerphone on the middle of the big desk. "And if I don't want to *share*?"

Levi's response was total silence.

"She will, Levi. She's just throwing up her defenses to figure out what to say without saying anything," Harrison snapped. "Come on, Zoe. Enough of this crap. We were shot at yesterday, and your father's dying. Your mother has round-the-clock security at the hospital, but what if that's not enough? What if whoever attacked her wants to finish the job?"

She slumped into the nearest chair. "Fine." She closed her eyes, sorting through the crazy thoughts in her head, took a deep breath and began. "I was home for the weekend. My parents had an argument over dinner. My father is an arrogant, egotistical man who doesn't believe women have a place in this world except in bed." She took another deep breath and continued in a flat monotone voice. "My brother was there that day, and so was I. The two of us never really got along. But at dinner that night, maybe because of what had happened to Tamara, or seeing my mom once again take my father's abuse, I snapped and to him to shut the hell up and leave Mom alone." She reached up and rubbed her temple.

"And?" Levi asked. "What happened after that?"

"There was an odd silence at the table. My father turned red, furiously angry. But instead of blasting me like he normally did, he got up and left the room. My mom rushed around to sit beside me. She put her arms around me saying, 'You have to run. You've crossed the line. You must go. Leave now.'" Zoe's voice faltered. "My father returned in a few minutes with a gun in his hand."

She refused to look at anybody as they listened to her. "All I could think then was he would shoot my mom. But now I think it was me that he wanted to put down."

"What did your brother do?"

"When he heard what Mother said, Alex laughed. He's no better than my father. He could be the next political asshole who takes bribes and picks up women, uses them thoroughly and spits them back out again."

She tried desperately to rein in her emotions. She locked her hands together in her lap, taking several deep, controlling breaths.

"When your father came in with the gun, what did your brother do?" Levi asked.

"He got up from the table and backed away. My father pointed the gun at me, but of course, my mother stepped in front of me. She was forever trying to save me from my father's blows." She shook her head. "Until I got strong enough to fight back. He stopped hitting me then, and with my threat to expose his actions, my mother as well, at least when I was around. But when I was absent …"

She stared at her hands to see blood in her palms from her nails fisted so tightly inside. She shoved her hands under her thighs and raised her gaze. "You have to understand what it's like to live with that kind of abuse. It's a day-in, day-out conditioning. I was raised with it from a toddler. By the time I understood how very wrong it was and how much my mother took from him, I could do very little. I left the house as much as I could because my presence made my father even worse. I hated boarding school, but if it made mine or my mother's life easier, then I went gladly. I took martial arts, and archery, shooting, and as much self-defense training as I could get my hands on. But none were very appropriate for a young lady, according to *him*," she said in a caustic tone. "No, we were supposed to do ballet, fencing, and Hostess 101. None of that prepares you for a father who breaks bones and damages so much more than skin and muscles." She shook her head. "The world didn't want to know about him. School didn't want to know about him. Nobody in my circle of friends wanted to know what he did behind closed doors." She gave a laugh. "My brother knew. He just didn't give a shit."

She hadn't meant to say all that. Once the dam opened, it all seemed to rush out.

"What happened when your father came into the room with the gun? After your mom stepped in front of you?" Ice asked.

"He waved the gun around, yelling at us both. My mom tried to calm him down. But he wasn't having anything to do with it. My mother told me to leave. My father told me to get the hell out and to never come back. I figured I was the fuel on this fire, and I needed to leave, so I did. I got up from the table, grabbed my purse and walked out."

"And again where was your brother?" Levi asked.

"He was in the dining room as far as I know."

"What the hell happened? What did you see? That wasn't the end obviously," Saul asked.

"I think my father probably put the gun down and used his hands to beat my mother." She shook her head. "You have to understand, he used her for a release of his temper. But he liked it. He loved to see her cower and cringe, broken and bleeding on the floor. She was his punching bag. You all know what it's like to work out and feel that power in your arms, fists, and legs as you kick and beat something to a pulp. That was my father. My mother and I were his punching bags. After just one of Father's beatings, Alex was forever saved. And I think that's because he had a penis, and the rest of us didn't." Her tone turned mocking. "I don't know if my mother shot my father. Honestly, if she did? Kudos to her. She should've done it a long time ago. Maybe she snapped and finally did it."

"And yet he was shot at the front door," Harrison softly

added.

Zoe leaned back. "Maybe? Or it could be a fabrication somebody made up to fit the circumstances. If this was my mom, I'm all for it. That bastard should've died thirty years ago. Hell, he should never have been born. As for my brother, he's just a weasel. Weak, but I don't think he's ever hurt anybody. He did try it on me once. When I was little. My mom stepped in and stopped him."

"He never tried again?" Harrison asked.

She shook her head. "No, he didn't. His torture became more subversive. He was much more cutting verbally. He liked emotional abuse and loved psychological. He used to come into my bedroom at nighttime, stand at the end of my bed and tell me my father was coming soon. I was a bed wetter until I was well over twelve." She shook her head. "The nightmares that I went through—knowing he was hovering just out of sight—they were brutal."

"Your brother is a sadistic asshole." Saul jumped to his feet. "It would be my pleasure to beat him to a pulp for all that shit."

She snorted. "You'd be the only one. He's the golden child. He could do no wrong, and my father wouldn't hear a word against him." She groaned. "But that doesn't mean Alex had anything to do with this either. He's not someone to get his fingers dirty."

SAUL MIGHT'VE LIKED a few minutes alone with her brother, but Harrison knew—if he ever got his hands on her father—the guys would have to make sure Harrison didn't kill the senator. And her brother? … Any guy who would do something like that to torment his little sister—who was already beaten and battered from their father—well, that proved Alex was broken inside. Apparently the men in her family had some major problems.

Harrison had seen families like that. He'd seen a lot of people spend their lives forgetting or hiding what they were. But eventually their masks slipped, they got cocky and relaxed. Their egos were big enough they believed they were safe. The trouble was, her brother was young. He had years and years and years where he could abuse other women. If he had kids, what would stop him from beating the crap out of them, like his father beat the women in his family? Not much.

He glanced around the room and said, "We need to find where Alex is and dig into his past a little more. He came and went at his parents' house, having his own room there, but we need more. We should talk to his associates, his neighbors, people he works with and for. And where else did he stay when he wasn't at home?"

Ice's voice came through loud and clear. "We can handle a lot of that from this end. You guys need to physically track him down."

"You're not listening to me," Zoe said. "I don't think he has anything to do with the attacks on my mother and father."

The men turned and stared at her.

She raised her hands in the air. "What? What is it you think I'm not seeing?"

Harrison shook his head. "He could be doing all kinds of things and not getting his hands dirty. Something inside could easily have snapped, and he could very well have been the one who carried out both attacks. But we won't know until we do some digging. Also what about the live-in staff at your house?" He looked at her. "We still can't get any answers from your mother."

Zoe reached her hand to her temple again.

He watched, seeing the fatigue, worry, and pain cross her features.

"Johan is the chauffeur and looks after the gardens and the yard. He also handles any tradesmen who come and go. Angelina works in the kitchen and around the house. She manages the extra staff who come in once a month to do a full clean." She frowned, wondering where they'd been when her father had been shot. "The two are married and have worked for my father for a long time."

"Children?"

She nodded. "Boys. Two of them. Fifteen months apart, both adults now. Neither live there anymore."

"How well do you know them?"

"I used to know them very well. But my father didn't think that association was a good thing. At that time, he sent them away to school. I'm sure it was to keep them separated from us. Even though we were in boarding school ourselves, our days off, holidays, never coincided. So I don't know where the boys are now."

"We'll add them to the list to check out," Ice said over the speakerphone.

Harrison gave her a few minutes while the rest of them set up schedules—who was going where, what they were to do. He turned toward the speakerphone. "Levi, did you get a follow-up from the cops?"

"Yes. A .22 handgun. Single shot to the head. The senator had an unregistered gun, but they haven't located it yet to confirm if it was the weapon used. And no staff was home to question. Harrison," Levi said, "get to the senator's house and talk to the staff. See if they can confirm any of this. And see if they have any idea where the brother is, what he's like."

"They're very loyal to my father," Zoe said. "They won't say anything unpleasant of course. They have a house on the property. They won't say anything that would cause them to lose their jobs and their living quarters."

"Because they still need the paycheck?"

She nodded. "Yet their relationship with my father was solid. But Angelina...there was something about her. She wasn't as friendly to me as she was the rest of the family." She shook her head. "Still I had little to do with them, so I'll keep my mouth shut and let you form your own opinions."

"We will," Saul said. "But anything you can tell us will help."

"What if the senator dies?" Levi asked. "What was the relationship between the pair and your mother? Is she likely to keep them on?"

Harrison watched Zoe wince.

"My mom is very generous and very easily taken in. She's already come from decades of abuse. Honestly, I don't think Johan or Angelina would be physically abusive. But they may be very manipulative to make sure they stayed where they were."

"They sound like real winners. What would you recommend your mother do when she gets home?" Harrison asked.

"I'll tell her to sell the house, get rid of the staff, move to a climate she prefers and start all over again."

"Is she likely to listen to that?" Saul asked.

She glanced at him and shrugged. "That is really hard to tell. My mother is very intelligent, but after thirty years of living with that level of fear, I don't know if she's strong enough to change."

Dakota asked, "Does she have any family? Anybody who could help snap her out of it?"

Zoe smiled. "Aunt Betty lives in Germany. She told my mom to get the hell out a long time ago. She's married to a German, and he told my mom to get out a long time ago too."

"But obviously she didn't listen. Any other family?"

"All four of my grandparents have passed away."

"Do you remember them?" Levi asked. "Did they have any relationship with the senator? Did you with them?"

She shook her head. "Formal dinners where I wasn't allowed to speak. I was only permitted to be seen at the occasional cocktail party where my paternal grandfather would show up. He didn't have any time for me either."

"I thought rich kids were to be envied," Dakota said. "But it sounds like it's a real shitty life."

She glanced at him. "You know what it's like playing in a playground, right?"

He nodded. "Sure, of course. Every kid does."

She shook her head. "I don't. I was never allowed to. I was never on a swing. I'm nearing thirty years old, and I've never been on a swing. I know that's a foolish comparison, but it should give you an idea. I've never been on a picnic. There were no sports days for me at school. There were no sleepovers at friends' houses or anything fun like that. It was all about academia, and, of course in the off-hours, it was all about drugs and sex. Because if you think boarding schools are anything other than the wealthy having easier access to all the above, you're wrong. Because they have oodles of money, are arrogant and egotistical, and really, if there is trouble with the school, the parents buy off the headmaster. Or pay a fee and the kid continues on his merry way. I used to sit and wish and wonder why I couldn't be in a public school where kids get to play hide-and-seek and tag and kick a ball around."

Finally, she held out her hands. "My father took my baseball and glove out of my hands. It wasn't *ladylike* enough."

Harrison sat back after exchanging a quick glance with the other men and realized he'd had no idea. "It's not something any of us thought about. We all had more or less normal upbringings. We did sleepovers at friends' houses. We did the usual Saturday morning play in the ballpark, rode bikes and generally hung out."

"Ride a bike? No." She chuckled. "Yeah, I've never ridden a bike." She opened her arms. "Not that I can't learn. But there is something very defeating about learning to ride a bike when you're almost thirty. I missed so many things growing up. And yet I had everything I could possibly want in many ways. I had the electronics. I had big fancy toys. I had a bedroom probably bigger than most people's top floors.

"But I was alone, and never allowed to have a friend sleep over because my mother was always traumatized. I could never have any friends in the house because my father was beating her up or in one of his moods, about to verbally attack me. Then, as I grew older, I didn't want anybody to know about my family. My house wasn't a home, it was a prison in which I chose to be alone because to have somebody there would be worse.

"If you really want to tear my family apart, expose all our secrets. Announce it on the news as ours being one of the worst families in the area. When I said, *I don't know anything else*, I meant it. I didn't have anything to do with my brother or father, and the only person I ever stayed connected with was my mother. And even that was very hard to do because she just wouldn't leave him. So I couldn't see her at home very often, and when I did, things like what happened the last time were always the result."

"That was not an unusual occurrence for you?" Levi said. "He would have these kinds of outbursts all the time?"

"Yes, but he never went so far as to bring out his handgun. I tried hard for my mother's sake to be the obedient daughter. Because if anybody paid, it would be her first. I made a point of always meeting her out of the house, even for coffee. But if he knew where she was going, it wasn't allowed either."

Harrison froze and said, "Then we really have to ask why you were there that night. You were actually staying at the house?"

She took in a slow jagged breath. "Yes. I was hoping to gain my father's cooperation." She rolled her eyes. "Foolish of me. I wanted him to help me with Tamara's case. So I was spending some days at home, looking for an opening to talk to him."

"You meant to use his power and authority as a senator to open a case or to have somebody take another look?" Harrison asked.

She nodded. "I was willing to take that chance to get justice for Tamara, but he didn't believe she'd been raped in the first place. I was hoping he would use it as part of his re=election platform. I needed somebody with power. Somebody who gave a damn, even if it was for the wrong reason."

"Did you contact the media?" Levi asked.

She nodded even though Levi couldn't see it. "A small

story published soon afterward in the local newspaper. Then I got an email about two days later, saying how the reporter had been fired and for me not to contact him again."

"Sounds like we have two very distinct issues here," Levi said. "Whether they actually cross, we can't tell yet. Harrison, I suggest you spend the day doing as much legwork as you can. We will conference again tomorrow morning, but I want an update tonight before all of you go to bed." Levi rang off.

Harrison asked Zoe, "You ready to go to the hospital?"

She stood, but he could see the fatigue pulling at her. The stress. She wrapped her arms around her chest and said, "Yes, let's go."

As they walked toward the front door, he asked, "Do you really think your mother would sell the house and leave town after your father dies?"

"She's hated that place since forever. And, yes, it's possible. I just don't know for sure. My mother has never been on her own in her life. I don't think she'd take to living alone easily."

"She must have friends."

"One of them is Richard." She smiled at Harrison. "She's talked about him a little. I have vague memories of meeting him. But never when my father was around."

Harrison nodded. "You never know. Maybe she'll end up seeing a little more of Richard when she heals."

"At least he's a nice man. He's looking after her. Instead of being the man who put her where she is."

ONCE AGAIN HARRISON parked behind the hospital, leading her through a secure rear entrance. He punched in the code, and she asked, "How is it you know them?"

"Richard texted them to me this morning. I was instructed to use this during the day only. We will be on camera from the time we enter, and before we get to the top floor where your mom is, they will have confirmed we're the only ones who came in and that we're going straight from here to there."

She shook her head. "I should be happy to hear she's under such intense security, but it's kind of unnerving."

"Unnerving, yes. But not a bad thing. Richard is making sure she's safe. And for that, you should be grateful."

"I am. That you are all ex-Navy is a huge help too."

He gave her an odd look. "Levi and his unit were betrayed on a mission. They were quite badly injured and were in the standard naval hospital. But we suspected somebody there was still trying to get to them. When the hospital was attacked, Ice quickly arranged for them to be airlifted out and had them moved here. So security is always tight now."

"Nice to have Ice to call on. Most people can't afford a medical facility like this."

"Exactly, but Richard is Ice's father, and this involved Levi. Ice and Levi have been together for a long time. Not an easy road, and at the point where this all blew up in their faces, they were on and off. However, as Levi healed, they got over their differences once and for all and are together now."

"Nice to see a light shining at the end of the tunnel for them." The elevator doors opened in front of them, and they stepped out.

Two security guards waited for them. Harrison nodded at them. "Any change in her condition?"

They both shook their heads. "She wakes and goes under."

As they walked toward Trish's room, the door opened, and Richard stepped out. He smiled at them. "Good timing. She's awake. I'll come in with you and see how her reaction is toward Zoe. See if there is any lucidity in her gaze."

Worried that her mother might not know her, per Richard's words, Zoe stepped cautiously inside her hospital room.

Her mother turned her head and gazed at her, and tears filled her beautiful blue eyes. She lifted her arms, and Zoe ran toward her. Crying, she dropped to the side of the bed and gently laid her head on her mother's chest. "Mom, oh, my God, you're awake."

Her voice slurred, she whispered, "I'm here, Zoe. I'm here."

Zoe's heart was overwhelmed with relief. She lay for a long moment, loving the solid thump of her mother's heartbeat, knowing she was now likely to make a full recovery. And, even if there was physical damage, chances were good that her mental faculties would return to normal.

When Zoe could, she sat up, snatched a tissue off the bedside table and wiped her eyes. She smiled at her mom and asked, "How are you feeling?"

Her mother smiled and let her eyes drift closed. "Like I've been run over by a cement truck," she whispered.

"Well, that's close."

Her mom's eyes opened. She stared at Zoe with a confused expression. "Was there a car accident?"

Zoe glanced at Richard, still standing in the room. She didn't know if she should say anything or not.

Richard gave her a slow shake of his head.

"No. We're not exactly sure what happened," she said, patting her mom's hand reassuringly. "All that's important is you're getting treatment, and you'll pull through."

She watched as her mother's eyelids closed again. She leaned down and kissed her mom's cheek. "I'm so glad to see you awake."

"So...tired," her mom whispered. Her voice drifted off, fainter and fainter.

Zoe rested her forehead against her mom's for a long moment, realizing that, as she did so, her mom had again been lured under into the peace and silence of slumber. She picked up her mom's hand and gently brought it to her lips. She looked at Richard. "She's gone back to sleep."

He softly patted Zoe on the shoulder. "But it's a healing sleep. She's been awake. She's managed to talk. She recognized you. Those are huge milestones."

Zoe smiled at him, tears once again forming in her eyes. "Please look after her."

He gave her the sweetest smile she thought she'd ever seen on the man.

"Of course I will. We're old friends."

Zoe stepped back, glancing at her mom. "Maybe when this is all over ..." She left it at that. For once her mother had to decide for herself. But it would be a long road before that happened. Zoe just hoped, if her mother ever found another man, it would be someone nice, like Richard. Nothing like her father. She glanced toward Harrison, standing at the closed door, waiting for her. She smiled and said, "It's okay. We can leave now."

He nodded toward her mom. "Richard, how long is she likely to sleep this time?"

"Most of the day again."

"May we stop by this afternoon?"

"I can't guarantee she'll be awake. I do understand you

need to ask questions, but she doesn't appear to remember what happened at this point." He held up a hand. "And before you ask, her memory will come back most likely, but it could take anywhere from a few minutes, days, or even weeks. Most of the time the brain blocks the trauma so patients have an easier time surviving. And right now, healing is what's most important."

Richard's phone buzzed. He pulled it out, and the color washed from his face. He turned a hard glare at Harrison. "Someone just tried to come through the same entrance you did."

"Saul or Dakota?"

Richard shook his head. "No idea. He wore a mask at the entrance but tossed it somewhere."

"How far in did he get?"

"He didn't. But he's searching for a weak entrance around the perimeter right now."

"Stay here," Harrison ordered Zoe. "I'll be back after I check it out."

"Really?" she snarled. "Remember who I am as well."

He turned to her in surprise before a look of understanding crossed his face. He leaned down and said, "I do. That's why I'm leaving you to guard your mother." He tilted up her chin and kissed her mouth. Hard.

Before she had a chance to react he was gone.

Chapter 9

ZOE RAISED HER fingers to her lips. If he had still been here, she'd consider decking him for that kiss. Or dragging him closer. *Sigh.* She was an idiot. She was grateful he remembered she was military too. It wasn't that she was infallible by any means. Part of the reason she got into the military had been to learn to fight. Learn more ways to defend herself. She'd taken enough beatings growing up. No way, no how, would she take any more. On top of that, she wouldn't let her mother suffer more either.

Security had gone with Harrison. Richard was talking on the phone. "Damn," she whispered. She glanced to the left and right. She had no intention of going outside or waking up her mom unless she had to. She took a quick assessment of the room, her mind cataloguing the differences, benefits, and weapons at hand.

This was a bedroom with a sitting room attached. It was comfortable, cozy, and relaxed-looking.

A huge advantage for someone during recovery. But not so much for anyone trying to cause chaos—or stop it. Anybody who studied hospitals for any length of time would know where the supply rooms were, how the laundry chute system worked, and where the disposable biohazardous materials were. Plus, the good or bad security in a place like this.

As far as weapons went, the room was looking more than scarce. And that was a real concern. She might not have the same training as Harrison did, but she was no slug. She excelled in every one of those defense classes she had taken.

Always with the thought of her father in the back of her mind. It was funny because none of the guys had asked her about that. She'd like to have beaten the crap out of him, like he had done to her. A bullet was way too easy, nice, and light a punishment for a man who had put her and her mom through hell.

Zoe walked into the bathroom. One bar of soap. There was a towel, however. She grabbed that.

It wouldn't help against a bullet. But if they came with knives, that was a whole different story.

A bathrobe hung behind the door. She quickly removed the tie and wrapped it around her wrist. She might not be strong enough to break a guy's neck easily, but she sure as hell could choke him to death.

She shook her head as she sorted through the room. She didn't understand why anybody would bother coming after her mother. It wasn't like she knew anything or was a danger to anyone.

Unless she had seen who had shot Father.

That was something worth killing for. Hard to consider her brother could've done something like this. But of course, anybody could have under the right circumstances. Then again, maybe her brother would have tried to take out the man who'd attacked their mother. She doubted it though, as she didn't remember him ever caring about her or Zoe. Alex was all about Alex.

Maybe he figured she'd give him a reward or sign over a big chunk of his inheritance as a thank you.

Zoe went out in the hallway to see Richard had left. At least he had security cameras in his hospital, and his security people were armed. She suspected Harrison was as well. She really needed to consider getting a license to carry herself.

She returned to her mom and sat at her bedside. She gently stroked her mother's fingers saying, "It's okay, Mom. I don't know if you're awake or not. But I'm here, and I won't let anybody hurt you ever again."

Her mother's eyes slowly drifted open. "I'm so sorry, sweetie. I couldn't stop it."

Zoe stroked her mom's cheek. "What are you sorry for, Mom? You don't have any reason to be."

Her mother made a tiny head movement that could've been either a nod or shake. "Yes," she whispered. "I should've left a long time ago."

"You don't have to now. He won't survive. The bullet is lodged in his brain. I haven't checked on him yet today."

That was a whole lot to tell her. But she knew her mother was worried. At the forming of a frown on her beautiful face, Zoe said, "I'll call and find out."

The frown cleared. Anything to keep a smile on her pretty face.

"Mom, you have to tell me. Who did this?" Zoe turned on the video feed to her phone, then placed it on the bedside table. This way she had a record of her mother's words. Maybe she wouldn't have to repeat the story several times to the police.

Her eyes flickered.

"You can't keep letting this happen to you."

"You don't understand. If I say anything, he'll come after you. Your father might not have shown you much love, but he didn't really want to lose you when it came down to it."

"What?" Zoe wanted to understand, to hear every little bit of what her mother had to say. "Mom, what are you talking about?"

"Two men came," she whispered. "Military men. Your father knew them both. There were harsh words, some laughter, then harsher words. Things got ugly."

Zoe sat straighter. "Mom, what about when Father pulled out a gun at dinner? I left soon afterward. Are you saying you didn't shoot him? Neither did Alex?"

Her mother's eyes opened. "Oh, no. I never shot him. I should've. Thirty years ago I should've, but I didn't." She gave a sad smile. "I was too weak to do that."

"So, after dinner, where was the gun?"

Her mother tossed and turned her head, obviously distressed.

Zoe picked up her hand and held it close. "Mom, this is very important. If you didn't shoot him, did he return to his office with his gun? Do you know if he put it away?"

"I don't know. I was really scared and in so much pain after your father's beating, I went to my room and stayed there. Then I heard the doorbell. I don't know if your brother let the men in or if it was your father. Alex left after dinner, but I don't know where he went. Your father's office is underneath my bedroom, so I could hear the voices and shouting." She fell silent.

"And?" Zoe urged. She was so close to getting some real information. Zoe needed her mother to stay strong. To stand up for something. "Mom, please."

Her mother raised her gaze. "I went downstairs. I heard the gunshot. They were at the front door, and I saw one of the men. I screamed. The young man, in a military uniform, ran toward me. The other called out and said, '*Leave her.*'"

Her mother's words were coated in such pain that Zoe had to close her eyes against it all. Against what her father had done to this beautiful woman—to break such a spirit of self-confidence to this ragtag female who nobody respected because she'd allowed herself to be beaten to nothing.

"Mom, you have to tell me what happened then."

Her mother opened her eyes and stared at her daughter. She reached up to stroke her cheek. "Zoe…"

She leaned closer until she could press her mother's palm against her cheek. "Come on. Tell me, Mom."

"I was already hurting from your father's beating earlier, but I couldn't ignore the shouting. Your father was in trouble. I heard the shot, saw him fall. Then the younger man saw me. He raced over and hit me as if he hated me for who, or what, I was, or maybe he hated all women." She shook her head. "I don't know. He hit me in the face, tried to strangle me. He kicked me." Tears poured from her mother's eyes. "The older man finally hauled him away and both left. But there was so much anger in him."

"Mom, this is really important. You need to tell me who these men were."

But the answer was heartbreaking. "I don't know. I never saw them before."

"It's okay. We'll find out."

Her mom shook her head, only to cry out in pain in the simple movement. "No. They told me to leave well enough alone, or they'd come back." She gasped as she tried to talk. "More than that, they said I'd never live to see you again, and I believed them."

"Mom, how old were these men?"

Her mom frowned, as if thinking back to her attack.

"One was older, like your father's age," she said. "He might've been the one who shot him." And she fell silent.

This was the part Zoe had to know, so she urged her mom. "Please, don't fall asleep until you tell me. What about the other man? How old was he? If you saw him, would you recognize him again?"

"He looked like the first man. It had to be father and son." And her mother shifted in the bed, quietly drifting off to sleep again.

Zoe heard a sound behind her. She jumped off the bed and whirled. A stranger stood in front of her, dressed in a white lab coat. There was a wary assessment in his eyes. She didn't know who the hell he was, or what he was doing here, but he wasn't medical, regardless of the coat, and he wasn't part of Harrison's team. If he was a security guard, he wasn't dressed for the role.

"Who the hell are you, and what are you doing in my mother's room?"

His gaze shifted to her mom and back to her, the tie around one wrist. The towel on the bed. But there was interest in his eyes. And something else, something dark.

"It's really too bad she lived." He took a half step forward.

Her lips turned into a grimace as she got ready to pounce if he took another.

"From the way I heard it, she was beaten so badly that she shouldn't be alive right now."

"She's a fighter. Unlike the asshole who did this. He hates women and thinks they are nothing," Zoe snapped. "He's all fluff. He can't take on a female who's standing in front of him. He has to wait until she's already broken, bleeding, and no real threat." She waited a half breath, then added in a hard tone, "Like you."

The man grimaced. "Unfortunately, you're quite correct. He doesn't fight fair in any way, shape, or form. Something you should remember. Not that you'll ever get a chance. But you're not my mission. She is. And I really hate to do this one because she's a fighter. I don't like this job. To have survived your father's abuse and now this beating—she must have a strong will to live."

"She does. She's been protecting me all my life. Even from assholes like you." From her peripheral vision she caught her mom's hand as she pressed the button to call the nurse. "This is a horrible job for you. You should really pick better contracts. I don't begrudge anybody a decent way to make a living, but there really should be some honor or standards."

He studied her for a long moment and looked back at her mom. "You know something? You could be right. I didn't like the sound of this one from the beginning. But the money was good."

"You can still look in the mirror in the morning? Is there nothing you won't do for a price? Who is your mother? Your sister? The one woman who you loved above all else? *This* woman has taken a massive beating. Where's the sorry excuse of a soldier who wasn't man enough to do his own dirty work?" Her muscles were locked down. But she had no illusions. Whoever this man was, he had skills.

He gave a half chuckle. "I can see you know who did this."

"I believe I do." She nodded. "A general and his son. The son did the beating. The general likely shot my father. But," she admitted, "I don't know for sure."

"What about you? How do you stay safe?"

Instinctively, Harrison's face popped into her mind. "I have people on my side. For once in my life, I'm not alone."

He assessed the distance between them. "I could've killed you half a dozen ways already."

She gave him a hard smile. "And I could've done the same. This is your one and only chance. Walk away, and don't come back. Leave my mother and me alone."

"What about your brother?"

"Did he have any part in this?" Her heart sank. *Please, no.*

A small smile faded from the corner of the stranger's lips. "Don't you know?"

She must answer carefully, her heart sinking with dread at his implication. She didn't know this stranger. She didn't trust him. But he had information she wanted. "My brother's on an ugly path. I don't know how far down it he's gone. He likes to terrorize women. He loves to watch them go to pieces. He's sick, twisted. But is he a killer? Did he shoot my father? Did he have a hand in my mother's abuse? I don't know," she said quietly. "I don't know if he can be saved at this point."

"That point is long past."

"So he *is* involved," she said, her gut knotting with pain.

"Maybe, maybe not," he said. "You're in trouble. You better have friends in pretty high places to keep you safe."

Once again she smiled. This time her mind flashed with the names *Levi* and *Ice*, along with images of all the other men she'd met so far who had stood up to help her. She inclined her head gently and said, "I do." Her tone was so positive, sure, and confident, there was no way he could have doubted her.

He took a step backward, nearer the doorway. She took

one forward. "How did you get in?"

He stared at her in silence but with a knowing look in his eyes.

"Somebody here told you about that entrance and the security codes?"

He inclined his head. "All information can be bought."

"Richard needs to go through his staff records to see who needs money. Time for a security change."

"In his case, he needs to find two of them. Because two people here are weak links in the system."

"And in my family, how many are there?"

By now he was at the doorway. He gave her an odd smile and said, "Everybody but the two of you apparently."

He darted out the door.

She raced after him, passing a nurse coming to answer her mother's summons. When she got to the end of the hallway, he was already gone. She wanted to chase him down. The best thing she could do right now was stay with Mom and commit to memory everything about him. Hopefully her phone caught most of what he said, but he was so far away from it...

Her father had been the bogeyman for her and her mom for a long time. And now she knew others just like him were after them. She pulled out her phone and sent a text to Harrison.

Contract killer was just here. Dressed all in black with doctor's lab coat. Age is hard to say, but from the way he moved, he was in his prime, so mid-thirties maybe. He's gone now. Richard has two on staff who were bought off.

Harrison's reply was instant.

Stay there. On my way.

OF COURSE HE had just done a full sweep of the place, and the intruder had been with her. At least she and her mother were okay. He left the other men standing outside, hoping to get the guy before he completely got away.

He blasted into Trish's hospital room to see Zoe sitting at her mom's bedside. Both were fine. He stopped, took a shuddering breath and tried to hold in all his other emotions.

She glanced at him and smiled. "He was actually very nice."

He glared at her. "How the hell can you say that?"

She shook her head. "I don't know. This whole business is making me crazy. What's wrong is right. What's right is wrong. I don't know anybody anymore, including myself."

"Did he have a weapon?"

"That guy didn't need one. He could kill in many ways," she said in a low voice. "He didn't attack either of us. We talked."

"Tell me what he said, all of it, right now."

Still sitting in the same place, one hand covering her mother's fingers, she clicked a button on her phone, and the stranger's voice filled the room.

Harrison's eyebrows rose, but he listened all the way through. He held out a hand so he could see any video she caught, but there wasn't much to look at. The phone was directed at the ceiling most of the time. Still the hospital cameras would have an image of him somewhere. "Description."

"Six feet, stocky, dark hair, T-shirt, tight black jeans, work boots—no, more like hiking." She shook her head.

"Hairy arms—if the backs of his hands are anything to go by. Lean face. His eyes…there was something about them. This job wasn't one he liked. I think he was happy to find a reason to walk away."

He snorted at that. "You really believe he's walking away from the contract money?"

She shook her head. "I know it doesn't make sense logically." She stared at her mom. "But I do know he likes fighters. And as far as he was concerned, that was what my mom was doing. He didn't want to add to her issues. He was willing to give her a chance to make her way through this."

"No names mentioned though?"

She shook her head. "No, but a father and son. According to my mom."

He walked closer and rested his hand on her shoulders—for his sake, not hers. He needed the physical contact to know she was okay. The last half hour could have ended so badly, yet it had gone extremely well. He didn't want to appreciate the guy, just her. But he had to. Because that guy could've taken out both women easily. Professional assassins had half a dozen ways to kill and then get the hell out. He'd chosen one path by leaving without doing harm. Harrison knew the hospital's cameras would pick him up. And that meant the guy didn't give a shit who had a photo of him. Or knew where all the cameras were. Either way, it scared Harrison all the more. He squeezed her shoulder gently and stepped back, then had a thought. Considered it a moment.

As he was about to go, she reached up a hand and grabbed his. "He did say he'd been paid a lot of money for this."

Harrison nodded. "They usually are." He smiled for the first time since he had entered the room. "I have an idea."

"About what?"

"I'm a bit of a hacker."

At that her eyebrows rose.

"If I can get Levi and Ice to work some of their magic, I may be able to add some of my own."

"Like what?"

He whispered, just to make sure Trish couldn't hear, asleep or not. "If I can make the contract money disappear, nobody's gonna do this hit."

"You can do that?"

"I'll sure try."

She smiled, tears welling, mouthing, *Thank you.* It took her a moment, but she found her voice again. "He also implied that my brother was somehow involved. He didn't come directly out and say it, but he basically said Alex was past saving. And how I wasn't safe and better have friends in high places."

"And we've stepped up the search for your brother," Harrison snapped. "Somebody has to have a lot of money to be hiring assassins. The fact that someone thought your mom was so close to death—and yet still had to finish her off—points to the person who wanted her attacked to begin with."

"My brother wouldn't get his hands dirty. He never has before. But he has money. I'm starting to realize he wouldn't have a problem paying big to make somebody else disappear." She stared at Harrison, tears in the corner of her eyes. Who and what was her brother? She'd never considered Alex in this light. And she didn't like it. "My own brother…it's hard to believe. He hated me, and I don't know why. He was disdainful of my mother, but I didn't think he hated her, just that he had no use for her. She was female—like me."

"We don't know that for sure yet. Hold tight. We will get the answers. Especially now that we have some idea where to go."

Richard leaned into the room then. He took one look at the three of them, and his shoulders sagged in relief. "Oh, my God. He was in here, wasn't he?"

Zoe nodded. "Yes, he was. And he said he paid two of your employees to get the codes."

Richard's face went white.

Harrison told Richard, "Levi and Ice are already working on that."

"Good. I want their names so I can report them. They won't be working in the industry every again." Richard snorted. "Very short term thinking on their part.

Zoe continued. "But he left, and I don't think he'll be back. He's no longer after my mom."

Richard closed his eyes in relief. "Thank God for that. I don't know what I'd do if she was hurt while on my watch."

"It still wouldn't be your fault," Harrison said. "This guy was a pro." His tone hardened like the snap of a whip. "Now who had the money to pay him?"

Chapter 10

"WE NEED TO talk to my brother," Zoe said. She pulled out her phone, clicked on his number and pressed the Call button. The number rang and rang and rang. She frowned when it went to voicemail and said, "This is Zoe. Call me back." She glared at her phone. "Where is he?"

"That's something to consider." Harrison leaned against the doorjamb. "Any chance the assassin has gone after him? Or went after him first?"

Her face twisted in a grimace. "Not a nice thought."

Richard said, "His face should be on the security cameras. My guys are looking right now." He pulled out his phone and called them. "Did you pick up an image of his face?" He listened for a moment, then turned to the others and said, his hand over the phone, "Nowhere in the hospital but in Trish's room."

He returned to his call and grinned. "Yes, send me a copy. … Please." Richard hung up the phone and pointed to the camera in the far corner of Trish's room at the top by the curtain. "He didn't expect a camera in your mother's room."

Zoe stared at Richard in surprise. "Neither did I."

"We'll turn it off when she wakes up," he said gently. "But, in her condition, I wanted to monitor her at all times."

Zoe nodded, but inside she still didn't like it. It felt very invasive. However, it was a good thing this time.

"I got it." Richard held up his phone. "You can't see it very clearly on the phone, so I'll send it to my tablet." Richard clicked on the tablet he carried in his lab coat pocket and brought up his email. He held it out for her to see. "Is this him?"

She studied the picture and nodded. "Yes, that's him."

They both looked at Harrison to see if he recognized him.

Harrison frowned at the image for a long time and said, "I think he's ex-military-turned-mercenary. But maybe he's taken a step to the left to become a private assassin."

Richard nodded, busily tapping away on his tablet. "Already sent it off to Ice. We'll also provide it to the police. They attacked here, and that makes it very personal. I want to make sure local law enforcement is included too. The staffing issue is already done."

"Does that mean they know my mother is here?"

"A few of them do. The police were brought in to the senator's house. She was supposed to go to General Hospital, but I had her rerouted and brought here. Obviously that meant I had to give a few explanations."

"Right." She shook her head. "I wish I'd been there."

"Maybe it's a good thing you weren't."

Harrison's phone rang. He glanced at it and said, "It's Levi. I'll be back in a minute." He stepped out into the hall.

Zoe glanced at her mother and spoke to Richard. "I had quite a conversation with her when she woke up." She explained the little bits she had gotten from her.

Richard shook his head. "I don't understand the mindset, where anybody thinks it's okay to treat another human being like he did her."

"She didn't actually see which of the two shot my father, but she said the older man didn't touch her. It was the younger one."

"But she didn't have any idea who they were?" Richard asked.

She shook her head. "But Angelina and her husband should know. The father-son pair shouldn't have been allowed onto our family's property without somebody clearing them through."

Harrison stepped into the room to hear the end of her conversation. "Surely they know what's going on now. We need to speak to that couple. We'll check your father's security cameras at the house too. If we can get an image of the two men, then we can track down who was your father's shooter as well as nail your mother's attacker."

"Then I'm sure the police would've collected the security discs already," she said. "Which is why I'm wondering if Angelina and her husband are a part of this."

"Time to find out." Harrison glanced to Richard. "You okay with the security as it is right now?"

He nodded. "After you leave, all the security codes will be changed, and my security team—vetted by Ice before I hired them, I might add—and I will be the only ones who have them. And for the moment"—he turned to Zoe—"we'll keep the camera running in your mother's room."

She nodded. "But please tell her that she's on camera. At least when it's safe to do so. I don't want her to have any setbacks."

Richard smiled. "We would never do anything to invade her privacy. This is entirely a security measure."

She nodded. "I hear you, but if it was me, I wouldn't like it."

His smile faded. He nodded. “None of us would. But she’s been through a lot, and her health is something we must monitor.”

She nodded, kissed him on the cheek. “You’re a nice man. I’m glad my mother knows you. When she wakes, tell her I’ll be back as soon as I can.”

As she passed Harrison, he muttered, “Watch it. You might be showing your feminine side.”

She shot him a hard look, then grinned. “I do have one.” She gave a half snort and turned away from him, then the two of them headed to the far hallway and the exit they had used to enter the hospital. “Are we going alone to my parents’ house, or are we taking your sidekicks?”

“The *sidekicks*, as you say, are in the parking lot, waiting for us.”

She greeted the two men as she hopped into the back of the Jeep. “Nothing like a little excitement to make the day go by faster.”

“Your kind comes with bullets though,” Saul said. “But the next asshole who tries to shoot my Jeep will get a surprise.”

She chuckled. “I’m fine. Thank you. Not that it matters that I spent half an hour talking with an assassin.” She shook her head in mockery and turned to look out the window. There was an awkward silence in the vehicle, and then she chuckled. “I’m just getting ideas for future assholes.”

Saul pulled from the parking lot and headed down the road, turning onto the main highway. “You have a mean streak,” he said, then smiled. “I like that.”

She snorted. “You guys have problems.”

Dakota chuckled. “That we do. That we do.”

They arrived at her parents’ house to find it empty.

There was no sign Angelina had been here, not for several days. Zoe walked through the place, deliberately avoiding looking at the bloodstained areas where both her father and mother had been attacked.

Putting a hand to her heart, she walked up the stairs to her bedroom, taking advantage while here to grab her overnight bag she'd left behind. Luckily she had never unpacked it. She had to be ready to leave here at a moment's notice. She had no idea where she would stay tonight, but she couldn't imagine staying here, at least not right now. If her mother needed her support when she got out of the hospital, that was a different story. But for now, she could really use some clothes. She grabbed her sweater and brought her bag downstairs, setting it on the floor by the door and draping her sweater over it. She found the others doing a thorough search of the house.

She should be upset they were going through everything. It should feel intrusive, but it didn't. She was more distant, more objective about this property than she'd realized. It was still her childhood home, but she'd left that behind a long time ago.

When she found Harrison in her father's office, she should've thought to check it out right away. "Do you see anything useful?"

He shook his head. "Lots of stuff about his position as senator. Was he a lawyer too?"

"Yes, but he hadn't practiced for many years."

He nodded, flipping through the various drawers in the large desk.

She walked over to the wall, clicked on the buttons, and the bookshelf pulled back. She heard Harrison let out a surprised, "Whoa."

He came around the desk and stepped up behind her. The wall safe was closed, locked. She tried the three codes she knew. None of them worked. She turned to look at Harrison. "He's changed the combination."

Saul stepped in then, looked at the safe, and his eyes lit up. He rubbed his hands together. "May I?"

She moved back and motioned toward the safe. "Be my guest."

Harrison turned to her and asked, "Any idea what's inside?"

"No, but I'm hoping my father's handgun is so the police can do a ballistics test."

"It will likely exonerate your mother. Because she didn't have access to any other gun. As far as your brother is concerned, I don't know about that."

She noticed how Harrison didn't mention her in that scenario of his. She realized her military background gave her the training to shoot her father and beat up her mother.

"Within seconds I'll have this open," Saul said as the tumblers fell into place. He turned the handle and pulled ever-so-slightly and backed up. "You may do the honors."

She hesitated. These were her father's private papers. She felt weird digging around in his safe. This was a man with dirty secrets. Knowing her father, he certainly never told her mother what he kept in here. Taking in a deep breath, she pulled the door fully open and studied the contents. Sure enough, inside was the handgun she remembered.

Harrison said, "Don't touch it." He reached inside with a handkerchief and wrapped it around the gun. He pulled it out, sniffed the barrel, took a closer look at her. "Doesn't smell like it's been fired recently." He laid it on the desk and snapped several photos before setting it aside. "We'll call the cops and let them know we found this and whatever else we may run across."

She pulled out a series of documents. A stack of money was at the very back and what appeared to be a jewelry case. She pulled the jewelry case from its perch, opened it to see some of her mother's favorite pieces. She smiled. "I'm glad she still has these. They were from much happier days. Several of these pieces are from my maternal grandmother."

She closed the case and placed it on top of the money, and then, with paperwork in hand, she sat. She quickly flipped through what appeared to be certificates—wedding and death—but found no surprises at this point. She got to the end where there were a series of photographs. Her father in his military years. He looked to be a much happier younger man. She wondered what made him so sour and dark in his life so fast. As she went through the photos, she saw the names scrawled on the back. She held them out to Harrison and said, "I don't know if this is of any use or not. These are records of his military career." As she studied them, she smiled. "So he excelled in the military as well. Who knew he was a decorated soldier? It's not something he ever spoke about."

She flipped through the rest. At the end of the stack, she came across an envelope. She pulled out the envelope and opened it, carefully dumping its contents into her hand. They appeared to be contracts or agreements of some kind. She settled back and studied them. There was a house deed but not to this place. She understood her father owned many properties.

She shook her head. "I really have no idea how big his financial holdings are."

"Normally a lawyer or a safety deposit box would hold a

lot of that information," Saul said. He turned his head, locking gazes with her. "There's an envelope underneath the money back here. Do you mind if I get it?"

She looked in the safe. "No, that's fine." She watched as he pulled out a maroon envelope and handed it to her. She opened it up. Inside was a card with a list of names. Beside it was a series of dollar amounts. She studied them. "I can't see my father blackmailing anybody, but I see this as a list of people who gave him money for no reason."

She handed the card to Harrison and checked the rest of the envelope, finding a picture of five soldiers. She shook her head. "It's probably nothing. Memories from way back when. Or that could've been a poker game where everybody owed him. For all I know, he cheats." She shook her head. "I should be kinder."

None of the men said anything.

She went through the rest of the documentation and said, "He has a lot of land and houses. But I don't see anything that indicates who might've shot him." She returned everything to the safe. She looked at the money. "That doesn't seem like very much money, does it?" She pulled out the two stacks of bills. "Last time I saw this safe open, there were at least ten of these stacks."

"Yeah, but how long ago was that?"

"Good point." She closed the safe, went to the bookshelf and pushed the buttons to put it back in place. "It was quite a few years ago." She glanced around the office. "We should probably come back here and spend more time, but I don't know what it is we're looking for."

On the wall were several photos of her father with many other men. But it was darn hard to know who the people were and what relationship they'd had with her father. "Let's go find the security tapes." She led them into the security room. It was simple, small, almost like a panic room. She'd been locked in here several times when she was "naughty." For that reason, she opened the door, showed them the system and stepped back out again.

Harrison glanced at her.

She shrugged. "It was one of my punishment places. I only destroyed the electronics once. After that, well, let's just say the punishment was severe enough it never happened again."

The men glanced around the small windowless room and shook their heads. Saul sat at the computer system and quickly brought up the date and time her father had been shot. But, of course, there was no tape, nothing at all from that date. "Before we determine somebody has removed them, we need to make sure the police don't have a copy."

"They should," Zoe said. "But the original should still be here."

"Let's not jump to conclusions," Saul said. "I'll run through the next few days to see if any other people have been here."

The tape started again the day before at noon. Which meant about fifteen hours were missing. They watched as he fast-forwarded, but nobody came in or out of the house. Including the staff.

She glanced at Harrison and said, "I'm getting a really ugly feeling about this."

He nodded.

"What if Johan and Angelina left?" she asked.

"You said there's a cottage out back. Let's see if they are there."

With Saul and Dakota joining them, the foursome

walked out the kitchen back door and followed the path to the small cottage. No vehicle was parked outside. They found no sign of anyone.

She knocked on the door. Nothing. She reached for the handle and pushed it open. The door slowly moved inward. And the smell hit her. She backed away, her hand over her nose.

"Shit." Harrison pulled her toward Dakota, grabbed his weapon from a hidden holster and entered the cottage with Saul close behind him. "Anyone here?"

She wanted to go inside, but Dakota held her firm. "Let the guys check it out first," he said. "Just because you're capable, doesn't mean you should."

She sighed. "It never occurred to me that they might be dead."

Harrison came out and said, "Two bodies—husband and wife, I presume. Are you up to identifying them?"

She took a deep breath and nodded. "Yes." She stepped inside.

Angelina had taken a shot in the forehead. She sat at the kitchen table, paperwork all over the wooden tabletop and a cup of coffee long gone cold. Her husband lay in the hallway, as if he'd heard the shot and had come running. He'd taken two shots, one in the chest and one in the head.

Harrison said, "Looks like they had a visitor. He stepped in and shot her. Her husband came running from wherever he was, and they took him down at the same time."

"I'm not a pro," she said slowly, "but that's what it looks like." She walked through the small cottage to their bedroom. There was no sign of anyone else.

"Can you tell if anything's been disturbed?"

She sent him a hard glance. "This is the first time I've

ever been in here."

The men were surprised at this, yet said nothing.

She shrugged. "You have to remember, nobody got along in my family." She motioned to the paperwork on the table. "There could be answers here though."

"Security cameras?" Dakota asked, his gaze studying the small cottage from the kitchen.

"No idea," she said quietly. She stared at the dead couple who'd been on the periphery of her entire life. A woman who she hadn't been close to but had been a part of her history. "We need to call the police," she said in a low tone.

"ALREADY DONE," HARRISON said. He put an arm around her shoulders. "Let's head to the main house."

Harrison led the way. She was quiet during the short walk, her footsteps slow, determined, but he could see—from her pale face and the fists she kept making—just how much of an impact two dead bodies on her family's property had made on her. But, of course, it should have. Whether she liked these people are not, they'd been part of her life.

"Any ideas?"

"Lots," she said in a sad tone. "I suspect the same father-son pair who shot my father. Tying up loose ends."

Harrison had to admit it flowed. It shouldn't be too hard to find out who had been here visiting. Then take photos to her mother and see if she remembered anything. But she might not. And, just because Zoe believed the man or men responsible for the cottage house deaths were connected with the men who attacked her parents, that didn't make it so. But, if it was, how many father-son military units where there? Harrison could get Levi and Ice to help pull names from the military database. But the police could do that too. Unless the military stonewalled them—depending on how high up the general, the father, was—that could also be a problem. "Any idea why they'd have fought? I know what your mother said, but is that reasonable?"

"It's hard to say with my father. In many ways, he was honorable. But in others, he was an asshole."

The last insult had been said in such a calm voice that he knew she'd been thinking of him in those terms for a long time. Then again, who could blame her?

At the house, they walked to her father's office again. She stopped in the doorway and looked toward the stairs. "I want to check my brother's room."

He nodded. "I want to see that room too." He glanced at his watch. "We probably have less than half an hour before the cops arrive."

"Fine."

Upstairs she checked her bedroom again, and they walked on down the hallway. She pointed out the double doors at one end and several single doors. "Those double doors are the master bedroom for my father. My mother's room has an adjoining door to my father's. And that first single door is to hers alone."

"They slept apart?"

"No. She was expected to be in his bed when he wanted her," she said in a cool tone.

"But she also had her own personal space."

"When he wanted it," she said.

They continued to a single door at the opposite end. "My brother wanted to be as far away from us as he could. This is the last room on this floor." She went to open the door but found it locked. She frowned. "I don't remember ever seeing any of these doors locked before."

Harrison bent, checking out the lock. Using the little tool pouch he carried in his back pocket, he pulled out a small file and played with the mechanism beneath the doorknob. Within seconds there was a *click*. He turned the knob and pushed open the door.

She looked at him and said, "We're not really breaking in, are we?"

"No." He stared at her. "Do you think your mother would object to this?"

"To find out who shot my father, beat her, and killed her long-time servants? Hell, no. And by rights, she could be the sole owner now."

"We should get an update from the hospital on your father."

She nodded. "I keep avoiding it," she confessed.

"Why?"

"Because, when I hear he's dead, I'll have to deal with all kinds of emotions and memories. But, while he's alive and restricted to a hospital room, I can push it away. If that wall falls, I'll be forced to face stuff I've refused to look at since childhood."

He looked around the large bedroom. "This is a huge room."

She nodded. "My brother never wanted any other but this one."

Harrison figured he could come up with an answer to that. He looked around. A very masculine dark mahogany bed, matching dresser, night tables and a huge entertainment center. Obviously old money in this room. He opened the closet doors. A lot of clothes hung here. But also a lot of empty hangers.

Zoe said, "He always left clothes behind. Mom said he was here sometimes for eight or nine days. Alex wanted one of the properties signed over to him." She shrugged. "My father was into control. I'm not sure Alex got very far. If he had, he wouldn't stay here as often as he did."

She said it in such a casual way that Harrison knew she didn't understand the impact of somebody handing over a house. So much of the world wished they could buy a house, and yet, here her brother was, hoping to be given one.

"Wow, you really do live in a different world." He went through the closet, looking for secrets. He figured somebody like her brother would have them. On the top shelf was an old childish-looking box. Like a keepsake box a mother would save.

He brought it down and took a closer look at school medals, report cards, and other childhood memories—like a couple favorite stones—things that meant nothing to anybody but Alex.

She glanced at it and nodded. "I remember seeing this stuff a while ago."

"Did he want to join the military?"

"Hell, no. He laughed when I went in. He said I was a fool."

"Of course." He walked over to the dresser, quickly scouted it. "There are a few sets of underclothes and a couple sweaters. But it's mostly empty."

He turned his attention to the night tables. One was completely empty; the other held a box of condoms. He glanced at Zoe. "Was he allowed to have girlfriends here?"

She shook her head. "No. Not until we were married, according to my father's rules. If we had sexual relationships, they weren't allowed in the home."

Harrison held up the box of condoms.

She looked at it and shrugged. "He's been sexually active since he was like fourteen."

Harrison replaced the condom box, looked through a popular novel sitting partially dog-eared on the nineteenth chapter. On a hunch, he lifted the night table and moved it off to the side. But nothing was behind it or under it. He glanced at the bed. It was big, ornate, dark and imposing. Nothing under the bed. He lifted the pillows, looked underneath. Nothing. The bed was on wheels. He pulled it out and checked behind the headboard and again found nothing. When he put the bed back in place, he turned around for other areas to search and found Zoe standing in the middle of the room, a curious look on her face.

"What are you looking for?"

"Anything. Something that says who he is, what he did when here and what he might do when not here. I'm looking to understand the man inside the room."

Chapter 11

SHE NODDED. "IF you find anything, let me know. I always thought he was hollow inside." She looked around, then hearing a mechanical sound on the other side, walked to the bathroom. She opened the door. The smell hit her first. She turned on the lights.

And let out a strangled cry.

Harrison raced up behind her.

A man in a military uniform was crumpled on the floor. A garrote had been used to take his life. It cut into the surface of the skin. His face was purple, bulging.

Harrison gently led Zoe out and away. "Stay back." He glanced again at her, making sure she was okay.

She had both hands over her mouth, staring at him wide-eyed. "I know who it is."

He glanced at the dead man and then at her. "One of the guys who raped your friend?"

She nodded. "Yes, but he never paid for his crimes as his father's high up in the military." As soon as she understood what she had said, she gasped. "Oh, my God! You think he and his father were the military pair my mom saw? That they shot my father and beat up my mother?" She dropped her gaze to the body on the floor. "Then what the hell is he doing up here?"

"Are there other entrances to this bedroom besides the

main door in the hallway?"

She nodded. "Several. He has a fire escape outside his window. He came and went often in the night."

Harrison nodded and glanced at the dead man. "From the looks of this guy, he was probably killed very soon after your mother was beaten."

"By my brother?"

"If he killed this guy in self-defense, he didn't need to run."

Then they heard the police sirens. Harrison grabbed her arm. "Let's go speak with the police. We now have two crime scenes. It'll be a very long night."

They stood on the front step as three police cruisers and an ambulance pulled up. She wrapped her arms around her chest.

One of the cops walked up. "Are you Zoe Branson?"

She nodded. "Yes, I am."

He said, "I'm here to arrest you for the murder of your father."

ZOE SWAYED IN place.

Harrison stepped up beside her and put an arm around her shoulders, while he pulled out his phone and called Richard. "Any chance Trish is awake? The senator must be dead because the police are here to arrest Zoe for the murder of her father."

Richard snapped, "What a travesty if they do that. I'll go check. I hadn't heard he had passed. Had anybody even told her that her father died?"

Harrison focused on the detective. "I don't think the police give a shit about the niceties of telling a daughter that her father has died. The detectives' only concern is getting credit for closing the senator's case."

The detective looked embarrassed. He turned to Zoe and asked, "You weren't notified?"

She shook her head, her hand over her mouth, tears in her eyes.

Another detective walked up, stood nearby.

She drew her hand away to speak. "But I don't think that matters to you guys, does it? I mean, I should be dancing with joy, because, as far as you're concerned, I'm the one who pulled the trigger."

Harrison could see the pain in her gaze. He turned her into his chest, where she buried her face against his shirt. He could feel the shudders rippling through her shoulders. "You can expect to hear about this from your superiors. I'll make sure a complaint is put through on this one."

The second detective said, "We're just messengers."

"So where the hell is the messenger who came to tell her that her father passed away?"

"We thought the hospital would've contacted her."

"As you can tell, nobody did," Harrison snapped. "We've been visiting with her mother and her doctor. Neither of them know yet either. So, when you do talk to her, make sure Richard, her doctor, is there. We don't want her having a relapse from your continued lack of tact." Harrison hugged Zoe tighter. "And, of course, Zoe will go with you willingly. However, we found two crime scenes on this property—three dead bodies in all, including the dead man upstairs in her brother's bedroom. *That* dead guy was likely the one who beat up her mother the night her father was shot. And *that dead guy's father* is the one who we think shot Zoe's father."

The detective frowned. "And what proof do you have? And what the hell do you mean that you've got dead bodies all over this property?"

Harrison quietly and calmly told him about Trish's statement. "We were here to collect more clothes for Zoe. We found a dead couple in the cottage on the grounds and also her father's .22 handgun in a safe in his home office. In her brother's bathroom upstairs is the third dead body."

The detective shook his head. "It doesn't change anything. You can explain everything at the police station."

Harrison watched as she drew away from him and stuck out her chin. "I'm not resisting arrest," she snapped, "but how stupid you'll look when you find out how very wrong you are."

"We were given a tip this morning about your actions. Somebody said they had proof."

"But, of course," Harrison said, "you wouldn't want real evidence from a real eyewitness, now would you?"

The detective frowned at him. "We haven't talked to her mother. So we're only going on your say-so."

"Yet you're here based on an anonymous tip, correct? Have you seen the alleged proof your anonymous tipster supposedly has? You do realize it was probably the killer himself who called in the tip, right?" Harrison asked drily.

The detectives exchanged glances. One of them asked, "Where are the bodies?"

Harrison pointed around the house. "There is a cottage at the back of the yard. Two are dead inside, a man and a woman. They were long-time employees of the senator. And upstairs is a young male dressed in a military uniform who, as far as we can tell, was the one who beat up the senator's wife. Mrs. Branson said his father was with him at the time.

We don't know which one or if both participated in the senator's death."

"Harrison, are you there?"

Harrison held the phone so the cops could hear. "I'm here with the police officers."

"I'm walking into Trish's room now. Trish? How are you doing, sweetie?"

Harrison noticed the softening of Richard's voice. They might be friends now, but it was a friendship that ran deep and strong between them.

Trish's voice was faint, but she could be heard through the phone. "I'm feeling a little bit better."

"I'm happy to hear that, but, Trish, I'm sorry to be the one to tell you that your husband died from his injuries."

There was no response from her. No sound at all.

"But now we have a rather pressing situation," Richard told Trish. "The police are at your house to arrest your daughter for murdering the senator."

Trish's gasp was audible to all. "Oh, my God, no! I told her who came to the house that night."

"The police aren't listening to her or anything she has to say. Can you talk to Harrison right now? He's with them and has it on speaker phone."

Richard must have handed the phone to Trish, who, in a shaky voice, identified herself. "Who am I speaking with?"

"Detective McKay and Anderson here," said one of the detectives. "We have a warrant for your daughter's arrest for the murder of the senator."

"Well, you're wrong." Her voice was fatigued, but she repeated the story she had already told Zoe. "As for the young man who attacked me, he should have been covered in my blood when he left. I know I was lying in a huge pool of it. So some of my blood must be on the uniform he wore that day. I hadn't seen the two men before, but my husband acted quite familiar with them. They were arguing."

"But you did not see who shot your husband?"

"That is correct. However, the only two people in the house, or in the yard, at the time were that man and his son."

"And your son?"

"I don't know where he was."

"But you were inside the house, not outside, and, therefore, you could not see if your daughter happened to be there."

Harrison felt Zoe stiffen in his arms. He wrapped her tighter in his embrace and held her still. He wondered if the police had a warrant for Alex too.

Trish's voice strengthened as she said, "I'm not a fool, gentleman. The double doors to the entranceway were wide open. Both men were standing there. There's no way anybody else shot my husband."

"But you can't prove that, can you?"

And Harrison knew exactly what would happen next. He whispered to Zoe. "You need to go with them. Don't resist arrest. We'll have a lawyer to you in no time."

She nodded, stepped away, turned to the men and said, "That's fine. I'll go with you. But I want your names and badge numbers. Because, when I take down that asshole from the military, I'll make sure I mention every one of you guys too."

The two men's gazes hardened. They nodded and said, "That's your right. But we have a warrant, and we'll carry it out."

Harrison could hear Trish calling out, "No, you can't arrest her."

Harrison held up one finger to the two detectives, wiggling his phone at them. "She can identify whether our dead military guy attacked her or not." He put the phone back to his ear and said, "Trish, I'll look after her. You stay calm and don't let this slow your healing. You're no good to your daughter if you collapse."

Richard's voice could be heard. "What do you need, Harrison?"

"First, a lawyer. The police are taking Zoe to the station right now. Second, I need Trish's help."

Harrison explained to Richard about the bodies on the property. "To add to both staff members being dead there is a dead man dressed in a soldier's uniform in the son's bathroom. I'll send you an image of his face. Have Trish look at it and see if she can identify him as the man who beat her up. Call me right back."

"I'll do that."

Harrison hung up. Moments later he sent pictures of the dead man to Richard, and Harrison's phone rang almost immediately. "Trish says it's him."

He looked at the detective in front of him and showed him the dead guy's photo on his phone. "So now go collect this asshole's father for his role in this too."

The detective looked at the ground. "I hear you. Things really stink in our department right now. And they're getting ugly fast."

"So pick a side, because when I take the lid off, a lot of shit will be flung in numerous directions."

The detective looked at him, glanced at his partner and said, "Sometimes we don't have any choice."

"You always have a choice." Harrison shook his head. "Every day every man has to make a choice where he stands. It's high time for you to make yours."

Chapter 12

SHE SAT, NUMB, in the police station. She'd been led to a table in a small room instead of being booked right away. That was a surprise. It was also a bit of a relief but not enough. She didn't want to go through this process, but likely nothing would save her from it. Nobody had asked her any further questions. Nobody seemed to give a damn now that they'd picked her up. While she could understand that, she still didn't like it. She was also surprised Harrison hadn't come with her. It stung a little.

The door opened. A bald-headed stranger walked up to her and said, "Zoe, my name is Lars."

She instantly felt no fear, even though he was huge and wore only one silver earring and that was in his left ear. She had never met anyone with that name before. She stood, smiled and shook his hand. "I'm sorry. I don't know you."

He gave her a gentle smile. "Maybe it's a good thing you don't," he said. "I'm a lawyer."

In an instant, her eyes filled with tears. She nodded, brushed away the wetness and said, "I didn't do this."

He patted her shoulder gently. "They can hold you for forty-eight hours, but that's it. Then they'll have to charge you. I'm not sure they will, given what Harrison has to say."

She brightened. "You spoke to him?"

He nodded. "Yes. We'll get to the bottom of this in no

time." He pulled up a chair beside her. "I'm glad you had someone helping you in this situation."

She nodded. "I am too. I wasn't sure my father's associates would handle it."

"Better not to involve them to avoid any conflict of interest. Plus they most likely don't handle criminal law."

She studied the lawyer for a long moment. In a low voice she asked, "Should I be asking about your fees? I don't have a whole lot of money."

He chuckled. "And you, a senator's daughter."

"The senator had the money. He didn't share. At least not with his daughter. His son, that was different."

"I do understand. But my fee is taken care. Now no more talk about that. I need to hear everything from you. Why don't you tell me from start to finish."

She winced. "When you say from the start, what do you mean?"

He studied her intently for a long moment. "Right now, from the day your father was shot."

She nodded and settled back in her chair. The telling took a little bit as she got in as much of the details as she could remember. Thankfully he recorded what she said. When she finished, she realized not only was he taping the conversation but he was taking notes.

"So you don't know who this man in the bathroom is?"

"His face was pretty distorted, but I think it was Paul Canley, the leader of the group who raped Tamara, my friend, and the one whose father is a general."

"Okay, now I need the rest of the story."

"Crap." She looked around for a glass of water. Finding nothing, she swallowed several times and said, "Here goes."

And she launched into telling him about Tamara—how

she'd been gang-raped in the showers and how Paul Canley had been the leader of the pack. "There were five, but two of them, Tamara said, Canley had forced to cooperate. It's like he was making sure all of them were guilty. Therefore, none of them would squeal." She shook her head. "Tamara was in a bad state. She didn't want to go to the medics. She didn't want to go to the police. I insisted she go to the hospital and be checked out. At the time, they did a rape kit. No semen was found, as far as I understand. Tamara did say they were all talking about using double condoms to make sure no evidence was left behind. Plus ..." She took a deep breath. "They cleaned her off afterward. She lay there, unconscious at that point."

"When did you find her?"

"I found her soon afterward. She was blue with cold, sobbing on the floor."

"What is the military saying about the case?"

"They say she liked rough sex, that she was well-known for having multiple sex partners, and so basically they tried her within their own minds and decided she'd asked for it," she snapped, then leaned back. "I'm sorry. There was more to it than that obviously. They said there was no proof these men were involved. As far as I'm concerned, they just brushed it all under the carpet and let the men go."

"And you think that happened why?"

She stared at him. "Because one of their fathers is a general."

Lars raised an eyebrow and nodded. "Being a general might help him in the military. But crimes at this level should never be covered up. And, yes, we know, the military polices its own," he said. "But it has to stop, and somebody must pay the price."

She leaned forward. "But nobody did because it was all processed internally. She was military. The five men were military. All of them were military. It was completely policed within the system. I don't know if she—we—had other options. I never asked. And I went the media route, but that didn't work out so well."

Lars nodded. "But now it seems the same perpetrators have taken it out of the military. They've attacked your mother and killed your father."

"Still there will be no justice for Tamara's death."

Lars looked up at Zoe. "Tamara's dead?"

That's when she realized she hadn't told him the rest of it. "After the rape, she was completely paralyzed with fear about taking a shower, even in her own bathroom. She couldn't be in the same room with the men. Everybody in the military knew. She had all kinds of guys coming on to her, making lewd remarks and suggestions. It was terrible. It was an environment of scorn and complete sabotage. Her self-confidence had always been high, but it became completely nonexistent. It was very painful to watch her go through it. I could do nothing but hold her hand and give her a hug. I kept fighting to get them to reopen the case, to punish these men. I did anything I could. *Legally*. Within the military's own rules. And they told me to shut up or ship out. I took the opportunity to ship out." She shook her head and stared around the room. "In my opinion, law enforcement is at an all-time low."

"Yet this was the military."

With bitterness in her voice she said, "They swore to uphold the law, to serve our country, protect those countrymen who couldn't fight. And it's a really hard thing to understand that, although they might have meant it at one time, they really don't give a shit in the end."

"I don't think the military is bad through and through," Lars said. "A lot of good men and women serve our country. But you get one bad apple running loose, and things go from bad to worse." He looked at the names she had given him. "Of the five young men, which one do you think was the weak link?"

She looked at him with respect. "That's a really good question. I'd say the last two names I gave you. According to Tamara, they were both coerced into participating."

"Did you speak with them?"

"Never could. They ended up telling the military I was harassing them."

"I bet Harrison could get them to talk." He raised his gaze to her and added, "Not to mention the fact that Harrison knows an awful lot of men in the military. His whole team does. Between them, they'd probably have several hundred people they could talk to. And if nothing else they might be able to prod the military into setting up a buddy system for the women in the armed forces – a checks and balance system."

She stared at him in delight. "When I think about Harrison, he'd scare anybody."

Lars laughed. "I don't think he'd take that too kindly."

She snorted. "He can consider it a compliment." She wished Harrison was here with her. "Can I get an update on what Harrison might've found?"

Lars nodded. "I'll let you know as soon as I hear anything."

The door opened, and somebody stepped in long enough to hand her a bottle of water.

"Do I have to retell all this to the police?"

Lars nodded. "Yes, repeatedly. That's why it's important to know exactly what you're saying each time and to not get caught up saying something contrary when they ask the same questions."

"I might be hazy on some of the details," she said quietly, "but I know the anonymous tip was a lie. Have I been formally charged?"

He chuckled. "No, you'd know if you had been. The police have various steps to the process."

"Hopefully, once they realize those three other murders on our property were probably committed on the same day that my parents were attacked, they will be looking for other suspects."

"Or," Lars said in a dry tone, "they will decide to charge you with multiple homicides."

"Oh, shit." She leaned back and rubbed her face. "I didn't kill anybody. Why are they not hunting down my brother and asking him what a body was doing locked in his bedroom? I am sure there are more security videos of the people who came and left my house too."

"It depends on what is on those missing security discs. Harrison is looking."

"Good luck with that. He needs to find them before the military does," she said bitterly.

"The police are likely to get them first. They have legal rights. But it's in your best interests to prove somebody was there other than yourself."

"Great. How do I do that when I'm stuck here?" She opened her phone's contact list. "This is my brother's number. I called, but it went to voice mail."

Lars wrote it down. "I'll send that to Levi as well." He sat back. "I forgot one part. According to Harrison, you also had a very interesting conversation at the hospital."

"If you call talking to the assassin who was paid to kill my mother *interesting* ..."

He turned the recorder on again. "From the beginning."

She rubbed her temples as she figured out where to start. "Richard told us an intruder had been seen at the same entrance we had used." It took ten minutes to get through that part as she recalled the conversation.

"Oh, wait..." She brightened and pulled out her phone again. Clicking on a button, she held it up so he could hear the conversation between her and the hired gun.

When it finished, she said, "I forgot I had that."

"And why is it that you believe he left without doing his job?"

"In a way, I think it was honor. Somehow it made him question what he was doing for money and whether he really needed to kill a woman who was already battered from so many years of abuse, and then knocked and kicked while she was on the floor. He really seemed offended by that. He made a decision she should live as she was such a fighter. Although he didn't say my brother had done any of this, he did say Alex had already gone down a path too dark to be saved."

"Then he knew of your brother's activities?"

"That's how I interpreted his comment."

Lars shook his head. "We have so much evidence right there on your phone. Give me a minute. Let me see if I can keep the police from charging you with anything. Can you send me that video?"

She nodded and sent it to his email.

"Now sit tight. I'll be back in a couple hours at the latest."

"When you do, would you bring me a cup of coffee?" she asked.

He nodded. "Hopefully I can take you to a restaurant to get food and coffee."

She gave him a bright smile. "In that case, forget the coffee. Just get me the hell out of here."

When he opened the door, two detectives stood in the hallway, waiting to come in. Lars smiled at them. "Good, I have something you need to listen to." The cops frowned at him but entered, Lars right behind them.

As soon as they sat, Lars hit Play on his phone so they could listen to the video, which only showed the ceiling of Trish's room because Zoe's phone had been sitting on her mother's bedside table while recording. But they could hear the voices clear enough. The cops exchanged looks, shook their heads and took notes.

She leaned forward and said, "I told you that I didn't kill them."

"But you didn't have any evidence to prove otherwise."

"Foolish me. I thought we were innocent until proven guilty."

The one detective who had been doing the talking rolled his eyes and said, "Now tell us everything."

She turned toward Lars. "Can't we just let them listen to your taped interview of me?"

He nodded, brought out his recorder and, over the next half hour, played the three statements she'd given.

The detectives looked at her. "We'll need those tapes."

She nodded. "Make sure all that goes into your police records. Because those asshole military men got away with rape, and Tamara was not the first or last."

The detectives shook their heads. "We can't do much

about the military."

She nodded. "I know that. Maybe I can do something about it with some help."

The younger detective looked at her, then at Lars. "Make sure it's legal."

"As legal as the military's judicial system is," she said, "which leaves a hell of a lot of leeway. Cover-up appears to be the system they operate under."

They winced. "Back to your father's case … we have a few questions."

She answered as much as she could, but the longer it went on, the more fatigued she felt.

Finally they asked, "What are your immediate plans?"

"I plan to meet Harrison at my house. Find my brother. Watch over my mother. And see if I can shake up some military brass and have a few of them get the shit kicked out of them or at least get them kicked out of the military."

The two men shared a look, then said, "We need contact information, an address where you'll be staying."

She handed over Richard's phone number, her own, and Harrison's. "I'm staying at Richard's house. I have no idea where it is. Somewhere in Morning Heights. You can call him and get an address. As for the rest on my plans, I need to figure out who I'm after next. You better find my brother." She brought up her contact list again. "That's his phone number. He needs to answer for the dead man in his bedroom. And, no, I don't know where my brother lives when he's not at home trying to get Father to sign over one of his houses to him."

The detective raised an eyebrow and said, "One of them?"

She nodded. "My father liked to own things. That included houses. Don't ask me what the address is. I don't know which house."

"Would your mother know?"

In a softer voice she said, "No, she would not. My mother wasn't allowed to know anything about the family business or holdings."

The men nodded. "We have to talk to your mother and confirm what she told you."

"Haven't you already spoken to her on the phone?" she snapped. "I can't have her upset over this. She needs to heal."

"That's true, but we must confirm that was her on the phone. So we do need to see her."

She nodded. "You must clear it with Richard, her doctor, first."

The men stood. One reached across the table and shook her hand. "Thanks for taping that conversation. It's a little bit of evidence that you have on your side right now. We'll hold off all charges until we get further information."

"No, you will drop the charges, based on the recorded eyewitness statement of one of the victims," Lars said and stood.

"I didn't have anything to do with this." She shot a hard look at the two detectives as she got up, turned and walked out.

HARRISON HOPED TO be at the police station in time to pick her up. Richard had kindly lent him the use of one of his cars, and Harrison was making good time. Except … well, he'd also hoped to be there in time to defend her. But he'd heard she was being released, so he was too late for that. The plan now was to take her to Richard's and keep her there. He knew she'd have something to say about that. But he wouldn't take her back to her house just to see the police everywhere. As crime scenes went, it was extensive.

There was still no sign of her brother. Nobody knew if Alex was alive and involved, or on the run and not involved, or dead and dumped somewhere. Harrison hoped there'd be closure in that area, but he could give no guarantees.

His phone had been going off steadily, between calls and texts to and from Lars, Levi, Ice, and Richard. Her mom was awake again and getting stronger. The message that the cops needed to talk to her had also gone through. The sooner that was done, the easier it would be on everybody, and it would stop the police from focusing on Zoe. If they couldn't believe the victim, then something was wrong with the judicial system. And it would also explain why the killers were making sure Trish didn't survive the attack. She knew who had done this. Since she was alive and getting stronger, the pressure would be even greater to take her out. Particularly since the initial hired gun seemed to have walked away from this hit. It didn't happen very often. Sadly too many others will step up to take over the job with the lure of big bucks.

That's what had tied up Harrison for so long. He couldn't very well hack into a murderer's secret bank account and dispose of his contract killer's fee while in a police station interrogation room, probably filled with cameras. While Harrison made the fee disappear, Ice had enlisted Bullard's people to track the money back to whoever had paid for the hit.

Meanwhile, back at the compound, Levi, Ice, and Sienna had drafted Lissa, Katina, and Alina's help with an old-fashioned phone tree implementation—done before the days of email; used by both PTA and soccer moms, basically all moms of any school-age children. So the six of them had their own list of about one hundred names each to contact via phone and to leave a voice mail only if necessary after three attempts. Harrison had his own truncated list of forty-seven to call, once he finished his hacking job.

The sole purpose of the phone tree calls was to set up an underground network to prevent these gang rapes and other hazing events that had gone on for far too long in our military branches.

Hopefully each of the six hundred contacts Levi had initially provided would reach out to another six hundred, who would reach to another six hundred, and on and on, ad infinitum. A pyramid scheme of the best kind.

And once Ice completed her call list, she hoped another of her computer runs would be done: a listing of every woman enlisted in each branch of the US military. She hoped to distribute that master list among their underground network and to get them busy matching up local overseers with each female in the Army, Navy, Air Force, and Marines. It would be a daunting task, but they had to start somewhere.

Plus, Harrison thought Zoe might want to lead a group—or reach out to survivors who would want to lead their own. That was her choice of course. He couldn't wait to share all this behind-the-scenes work they had done. But she had enough on her plate at the moment, so he'd wait, after things calmed down here first.

He pulled into the parking lot behind the police station in time to see Lars walking out the side door with Zoe. She looked exhausted and yet brighter. He tooted the horn and pulled up beside them, rolled down his window and told Zoe, "Hop in."

She looked at him and asked, "Where's the Jeep?"

"Running backup as usual."

Instinctively she looked around for it, then turned to Lars. "Thank you."

He responded with a smile and a wave of his hand. "No problem. Keep me in the loop."

She nodded, then walked to the passenger side of Harrison's vehicle and got in. She was still amazed how somebody so big and so badass-looking as Lars could have such a gentle smile.

Harrison waited until she buckled up, then pulled from the parking lot. "You doing okay?"

"I am. I hope to never be in a position like that again." She shook her head. "And I'm still not off the hook. It's like they want to believe me, but, at the same time, it's hard letting go of their very promising lead. Because if they don't have me, they have nothing."

"That might've been true before, but now, with the extra bodies, plus your recording, they have a ton more forensic evidence to follow up on. They will get the bad guys. Don't you worry."

She snorted. "I'm running a little low on faith."

"Not everybody's a bad guy." He pulled into the mainstream traffic, changed lanes and took the next turn off to the right.

"Where are we going?"

"To Richard's."

She shook her head. "I want to see my mom first. I'll sleep better knowing she's okay."

Seeing her fatigue but also her need to connect with someone from her world who loved her, he said, "Call Richard. We need his permission, and he needs a heads-up."

Using her phone, she dialed Richard. When he answered, she explained her request.

"Of course you can see her. She's awake and has been asking for you. I'm really glad the police released you."

"Thank you," she said in a choked-up voice. She glanced at Harrison. "How long?"

"Ten minutes."

"Did you hear that?" she asked Richard.

"Yes, ten minutes. I'll set it up."

She ended the call and put her phone in her lap. "Anything new about the victim found in my brother's room?"

"Positively identified as you suspected. It's Paul Canley."

"Well, at least justice has been served on one of them."

At her words, he turned to look at her. "Please tell me that you had nothing to do with this."

She looked at him in surprise. "Of course not. I wanted them punished, not dead."

"With good reason."

Slouching in her seat, she yawned. "I could sleep for a week."

"After your visit with your mom, we'll go to Richard's, get you some food and put you to bed." He reached a hand across the front seat and held it open, palm up. When she didn't hesitate to place her much smaller one into his, he could feel something settle inside. Something good. Right. Honest. He didn't want her to think he doubted her. She needed to know he was on her side, firmly and forever. She'd been given a lot of bad deals in this world, taken some serious hits. But not all of life, and not all people, were bad.

He wanted her to see him in a completely different light. Not as a bodyguard but as a friend—or something more than a friend. He hadn't really believed in *instant* love, although he certainly believed in instant sex, because, hell, that was the modern relationship for those who couldn't do *forever*. He didn't have a problem with that if everyone was available and willing. He looked at the tired but valiant warrior beside him—still so angry, prickly, and against the world—and he realized he'd been looking for the wrong kind of woman. He'd always chosen soft and weak. He didn't really think of those women as weak, but they wanted different things. Those women had always been the kind who would've deferred to him, not faulted him when he was wrong. They would always back away when his own back got up. Instead, this woman beside him would shove her face in his and tell him to back down.

And he needed that. It wasn't something he'd realized before, but he really did need it. He didn't want a doormat. He wanted somebody feisty, someone to partner with, not someone to look after constantly. He wanted to grow old with the same person. He envisioned him and Zoe sitting in two rocking chairs on their porch at seventy to eighty years old. She would never put up with his crap. She'd always dish it right back to him.

It wasn't like he had a confrontational personality, but he didn't want someone who would back off and make him feel like he was threatening them, because it wasn't in his nature to threaten—unless he was dealing with bad guys. But, if he got blustery and loud with his lover, he didn't want her to cower. With Zoe, there would be no cowering. She was too damn busy snapping back at him.

"What the hell are you grinning about?" she growled.

At her tone, his grin widened. "I've decided I like turtles," he announced. Followed by silence.

She stared at him with confusion on her face. "That's

nice." She rolled her eyes and settled into her seat, resting against the car door.

He chuckled. "Snapping turtles in particular." As he caught her glare, he realized she was catching on.

"Better than having too much sweetness in life."

"I'm sure you were nice, sweet, and cuddly at some point in your life," he said. "But you certainly aren't right now. Nor have you been since I met you. But that's what I've decided I like. Porcupines, snapping turtles, and she-bears."

She sat up. "I'm not that bad."

At that, he really chuckled. When his laughter died down, he saw her staring at him, and, dammit, hurt was in her eyes.

In a low voice, she asked, "Am I?"

He shook his head. "Nope, you're not. You're about the perfect amount of snapping and snarling. And you're not pretending to be someone else. After a few months being with that kind of person, I'd be disappointed to find out it was all a facade."

"I don't put on airs—anywhere. That drove my mother nuts. I always figured it was better to be me and honest."

"I agree with that."

"And I'm not always like this," she said quietly. "Some of it resulted from Tamara's death. I got so angry. I had no outlet for all that sense of injustice, and I could find no peace."

He squeezed her hand gently. "There are always life-changing events. How we react, how we deal with them, how we move forward in life is the trick. It's not easy but so worth doing. And good for you for feeling that sense of injustice on Tamara's behalf. It was a horrible time in your life. But you did the best you could. Now some of us who have more power, or who know certain people, will do what we can. Still we can't guarantee justice for her, but we'll try."

She squeezed his fingers. "Thank you."

He pulled into the hospital parking lot and drove around to the back. They got out and headed to the same exit they'd used before. Harrison punched in the new code Richard had texted them, then waved at the security camera, and the door unlocked in front of them. They walked in, and it closed. He could hear security changing the codes behind them.

"Richard's not taking anything for granted, is he?" Zoe asked.

"No, not after the last intruder."

They walked upstairs without seeing anyone. When they reached the top floor, they found two security guards waiting for them as usual. As soon as they were cleared, they walked to her mother's room. Two more guards were stationed close to Trish's door.

Zoe visibly calmed down when she realized her mother really was protected. "Does Richard do this for everyone or only for my mom?"

"Probably for anybody who needs it, but, I think, in this case, your mom has a special place in his heart."

She gave Harrison a smile. "Yeah, I don't think Mom will be alone for too long now. Richard is a good man. I can't ever see him beating the crap out of her."

"No, he's not your father."

They walked in the door to see her mother sitting up in bed, a small table over her lap, enjoying a cup of tea. As soon as she saw Zoe, her face lit up. Harrison could finally see the shadow of the beauty Trish must be when her face wasn't puffy and purple.

Zoe ran to her side, gently leaned over and gave her mom a hug. "You're looking so much better."

"I'm feeling much better." She patted her daughter's hand and searched her face. "I must say though, you don't look well."

Zoe gave Harrison a look and said, "It's been a bit of a rough day."

Her mother nodded. "Richard explained. I'm so glad the police let you leave." Trish turned her head toward Harrison and gave him a small smile. "Where are my manners? You must be Harrison."

"Yes, ma'am." He took one step closer.

"Thank you so much for helping my daughter through this."

"My pleasure, ma'am."

"Mom, we have to find Alex." She couldn't explain why to her mother. Not while she was still recovering.

"I have no idea where he is." But her gaze looked to the side.

"Mom, did Father give Alex one of the houses?"

Her mother winced and said, "I don't know for sure if it went through."

"And you didn't want me to know because there was no house for me, correct?"

Her mother nodded. "I don't know why your father never treated you fairly."

"Well, it doesn't matter anymore because he's not alive now to physically dish out his particular prejudices."

"There'll be lots of paperwork to deal with yet," her mother said. "I'm not even sure what financial holdings there are."

"Or that he left anything to you," Zoe warned her

mother. "Father was nothing if not very closemouthed. It's quite possible he would turn it all over to Alex."

Her mother shrugged. "To be finally free of all that physical terror and the nightmares, it'll be worth it."

Zoe sat back, a big smile on her face. "Good, that's the attitude. I can always find a job and support the two of us."

Her mother patted her cheek. "I have some money of my own. Don't you worry about me. I won't live in the style I was used to, but, on the other hand, I'll be safer, happier, less afraid."

Zoe smiled. "As long as you're safe and sound, and the police find these terrible men, it'll all be good."

Harrison listened to the exchange with interest. He saw a wealthy woman cheerfully trading her moneyed lifestyle she'd always lived to have a simpler one now that was peaceful and without constant pain and terror. And he really appreciated how Zoe had willingly stepped up with her offer to support them both, though he had no idea how or what she would do. She didn't have a full-time job. But they were an interesting mix. Both women were survivors. And, as such, although they could *use* help, they didn't *need* it from anyone in their lives. He felt he should leave the room and give them some privacy.

His phone rang at that thought. He pulled it out and saw it was Saul. He motioned to Zoe, saying, "I have to take this." He stepped outside and answered the call as he walked down the hallway. "What's up, Saul?"

"Dakota's been shot."

Chapter 13

ZOE LOOKED UP as Harrison stepped inside her mother's hospital room.

His face was hard, locked down.

Instantly she knew something bad had happened. She bolted to her feet and ran to him. "What's wrong?"

"Dakota's been shot."

"Oh, dear God." She threw her arms around him. "Is he alive? How bad?"

Harrison hugged her up close.

She couldn't give him comfort up until now. It had been him helping her to this point. She stared at his face to see his ravaged expression. "Is it that bad?"

"He's in surgery. I don't know how bad it is."

"Do you know who shot him?"

"Not yet," Harrison snapped. "But we will soon." He shook his head. "Sorry, I didn't mean to snap at you. I'm heading straight to the hospital."

She reached out to stop him. "I know that's what you want to do because he's your friend. But he's in surgery. Probably for hours. You can do nothing for him right now. Let's be reasonable about this. Is there anything we can do to catch the guy who shot him?"

He stared at her, a muscle twitching in his jaw. She could see him battling the present reality against his emotional needs. Then he nodded. "I'll call Saul first. Stay inside this room."

She stepped back but watched him as he walked up and down the hallway, his phone to his ear.

When he was done, he turned to her. "You should stay here with your mom."

She shook her head. "No. I'm coming with you." He opened his mouth, but she placed her index finger against his lips. "No. Don't even bother arguing." She glanced at Trish. "Mom, I'll call you later. Stay safe."

Her mother gave her a wan smile. "It's probably good that you're leaving right now. I'm feeling really tired again."

Zoe ran back inside, gave her mom a gentle hug and a kiss, and whispered, "Sleep. Just sleep."

She dashed from the room to see Harrison already walking toward the stairs. She rolled her eyes and ran to catch up with him. She hooked her arm through his and tried to keep up. She was short and small; he was tall and big. And those long strides of his made her run. The last thing she would do was complain. Like hell that would happen now.

She raced down the stairs, keeping up with him. Outside, she quickly jumped into the passenger seat of the car he'd picked her up in earlier. "What did Saul have to say?"

"He's downtown. He has the shooter pinned inside an old house. He's called the cops for backup, but they don't have anybody available for like twenty minutes."

"See? It was a damn good thing you didn't go to the hospital first. Saul needs you."

Harrison didn't say anything. But, with the engine now running, he roared from the parking lot, hit the main road and punched the address into the GPS. Within minutes, they were almost there.

"We're not very far away at all," she said in astonishment. "I wonder what Saul and Dakota were doing?"

"They had followed us to the hospital, and then they were checking a few addresses Levi had found."

"Then who the hell took Dakota to the hospital if there are no cops available? And how did Saul get the guy pinned down?"

"I'm not sure on all the details, but Saul mentioned soldiers were involved, so we must be prepared." He turned a corner. "The address is for one of those names on your list."

She gasped. "That's terrible." She shook her head. "We have to find those two men, the weak links in Paul's network."

"Maybe we'll track them down after this."

He roared up the street and parked several houses from the address on the GPS. He looked at her. "Since you're not armed, you should stay in the vehicle."

She watched as he bolted from the car and raced toward Saul, hiding in the cedars behind a neighbor's house. She could see the two men talking before Harrison creeped along the fence and went to the rear of the house in question. She might not be armed, but she wasn't helpless.

She left the car and raced up to Saul. In a low voice she said, "I'll stand watch. Go. We don't want Harrison to enter that house without backup."

Saul gave her a hard look, appeared to like what he saw and pulled a gun from his boot, handing it to her. "According to Harrison, you're ex-military. So you know how to use this."

She accepted the weapon with relief and nodded. "Go. Look after Harrison."

He was gone. She stood watch, her phone in one hand,

gun in the other. She waited for the two men to enter the back. If they flushed somebody out the front, she had no problem putting a bullet in the runner. Especially if it was one of the assholes who had raped Tamara. She had to make sure she was justified in the shooting and that she aimed to maim not to kill. She wouldn't go looking for an opportunity to shoot, but, if any runner didn't stand down, well, that was his problem.

She watched, soon hearing shouts, noises, gunfire, return fire, then the front door slammed open, and a man came barreling down the stairs. He was armed. He turned and fired through the front door. She raced up to the gate at the fence and held the gun on him. "Stop or I'll shoot."

The man turned to face the new threat, recognized her, and a snarl ripped through his features. "You're on, you fucking bitch. You've been nothing but goddamn trouble." And he raised his weapon and fired.

Saul was correct. She was military trained, and she fired off the first shot. It took everything she had not to shoot to kill. But, in the long run, she wanted this asshole to suffer in prison for one hell of a long time. She had taken out his gun hand, shooting between his fingers, ripping through his wrist. It would certainly destroy his right arm for a long time to come.

He screamed, dropped the gun and stood there, blood dripping from his shattered hand.

She stepped up and kept her weapon trained on him. "Down on the ground, Jeff," she yelled.

He snarled at her and crouched as if to attack.

She lowered the gun, pointing right at his crotch. "I don't give a shit if you have any balls or not when you are in prison. But maybe it's a good thing if you don't. You're gonna be somebody's bitch for a long time."

He stared at her, his mouth working as if he wanted to fight, but Harrison and Saul were now out of the house, standing beside her.

Harrison pulled Jeff's good hand back. He lifted up Jeff's bleeding hand and said, "Don't you know anything about looking after injuries like this? Keep it raised. It helps the bleeding to slow down." His voice was mocking and hard. He had his phone out, calling the cops.

With Saul's gun leveled at Jeff, Zoe slowly lowered her weapon. She was a little shaky. She returned the gun to Saul and said, "You should be proud of me. I really wanted to shoot off his balls." She paced the sidewalk, working out some of her tension, watching the men deal with Jeff. Then she approached him again. "I presume Randy and Lee took the man you shot to the hospital?"

"I didn't shoot him." He glared at her.

She turned away, and then whipped out her foot and kicked the elbow of his injured arm.

He screamed so loud he could be heard all around the neighborhood.

"Oh, look at that. Your girlie scream will get the cops here a whole lot faster." She glared at him and said, "Do you really think I give a shit what happens to you?"

"You should, bitch, because I'll make sure something nasty happens to you," he taunted.

"Yeah, big tough guy who has to rape a woman as part of a gang. Why is that? Is it the only way you can get a hard-on? The military can't protect you anymore, you know? You shot a civilian."

He sneered.

She stopped, then nodded. "Right. It was likely Lawrence who shot Dakota. If the three of you were here, then he was too."

"It was self-defense, bitch."

"Yeah, what about my mother?"

He frowned in confusion. "I don't know about your damn mother."

She studied him. "What about my father?"

He shook his head. "I don't know what the fuck you're talking about."

"Nothing other than the rapes? So you weren't part of shooting my father or beating up my mother? Or how about the two people who worked for my father who were shot and left for dead in the cottage?"

Again he shook his head. "What the hell are you talking about? You're not blaming any of that shit on me. I didn't have anything to do with any of that." He glared at her. "I don't know anything about murder. Stupid bitch. You should never have been in the military in the first place."

Harrison pulled out his phone, flipped through the photos and held up a picture. "What about this man? He was your best buddy, right? The one you raped women with? Are you guys part of some brotherhood bullshit? You know he's dead, right?" He held the photo closer so Jeff could see the bloated face of the man they'd found in Alex's bathroom.

Jeff's face turned stark white. "Shit. I don't know anything about that. Look to her for that. Jesus Christ. She's probably picking us off one by one." He turned his gaze away, looked back and said, "What happened to him?"

"Someone garrotted him," Zoe said. "I figured you did it for sure."

"What? No. He was my best friend. I didn't know he was dead. I haven't talked to him in the last couple days." He shook his head. "I haven't talked to him in like a week. Maybe longer, I don't know. His father was pestering him for being in trouble a lot, so we gave it a bit of a break."

"Pestering him about what?" she snapped.

He shrugged. "The military didn't like all the problems. They considered you a troublemaker, but your campaign had raised a lot of attention."

"Instead, this father and son duo was at my father's house, shot him and then beat my mother within an inch of her life."

He sagged in place. "Look, I don't know anything about that, okay? So we had fun with some women in the military. They all wanted it. They all knew exactly what they were getting into when they enlisted. I'm so goddamn tired of all these women crying rape afterward." He shook his head again. "Fucking bitches."

"Was that Paul's attitude too?"

"Of course it was. Paul usually got the women. He made all the arrangements."

"Well, Paul's dead now. So he can't defend himself anymore, which is a good thing because I'd probably punch him out if he tried. And now we're looking for his father. Of course, Jeff, we're also looking for the other three rapists. There were five, right?"

He sighed, then nodded. "Believe me, Randy and Lee didn't want to do it." He snorted. "Honestly I'm not sure they did it with her. They're both gay. I know Randy couldn't get a hard-on with Tamara."

"How nice to be thankful for some things," she said caustically.

He shrugged. "I wouldn't be at all surprised if those two didn't rat us out. They were here for a while, but then they disappeared. As for Lawrence, I have no idea where he is. He was here, shot the guy and disappeared. I haven't had much to do with him since the shit hit the fan over Tamara's suicide, and the group broke up."

"Did the general save your ass in the military too?"

"He had to. If he didn't protect me, I could've taken Paul down in a heartbeat."

"And how many women did you do this to … what you did to Tamara?"

He shrugged. "You can't compare them to Tamara. I don't know what the hell that was all about. She was all over Paul at the beginning."

"Because she may have wanted to date Paul didn't mean she deserved to be raped by all of you." She stared at him in disgust. "How many other women?"

"A couple. I don't know—maybe four or five. Nobody made any stink about it like Tamara did."

"Names." In the distance, she heard sirens. She pressed, "I want the names of all the women."

"You can ask all you want, bitch."

Harrison grabbed him by the scruff of the neck and pinched real hard.

Jeff gargled a funny noise, like the oxygen was cut off to his windpipe. When Harrison released him, he gasped.

In a conversational tone, Zoe said, "One way or the other you're doing jail time. For all I know, you're involved in my mother's beating and in my father's murder. And, as far as I can see, you likely had something to do with Paul's murder too."

He stared at her in horror. "I didn't have anything to do with any of that shit."

"The women's names." Her voice was hard.

He closed his eyes and recited them.

She'd heard of one, knew of another, but the others were new. She nodded. "You sure there are no others?"

He shook his head. "No, there were no others. Paul might've done a few on his own, but we didn't do any more together."

"What about the two of you without the gang?"

He shook his head. "No, we figured there was safety in numbers."

"Thus proving you knew it was wrong from the beginning."

"I'm not saying another fucking word to you, bitch."

She shrugged, holding up her phone to him. "It doesn't matter if you do or not. I already taped this conversation." She raised her gaze to Harrison. "Thank you."

He inclined his head. "We'll make sure all of them go down."

"I want justice," she said. "Even though it's too late for Tamara, it's not for those other women to know they are not forsaken because they don't have a penis." She shot a hard glance at Jeff and said, "I'd sure like to nail some of the murders on you, making sure you do plenty of jail time and are somebody's bitch. See how you like the showers after you're gang-raped." She turned and walked along the sidewalk, pacing back and forth again. She had to clear her head. It was one thing to pick up the three other men, but what the hell did all this have to do with her brother?

She returned with more questions for Jeff. "Do you know my brother?"

He shook his head, his face pale as the shock of his injury kicked in. He collapsed to his knees, his bloody hand gingerly against his chest. "I know *of* your brother. Paul knew him."

"Did you know Paul was meeting him?"

"They met off and on for years." He snorted. "Your brother is bad news."

"I know." She nodded. "I just don't know how bad."

He stared at her in surprise, sweat pouring off his forehead "He's way worse than Paul."

"You have any proof of that?"

"Proof? Paul sure as hell did," he snapped. "He liked to have things on different people. I think that's why his father was forced to protect him. Paul had stuff on his own father."

"Nice family."

"Almost as nice as yours," he shot back.

She winced. "Good point."

AFTER THE COPS arrived, Harrison made a quick phone call, sharing updates with Levi. Harrison learned the ballistics on the senator's gun confirmed he hadn't been killed with it. When Harrison was done, he walked over to the same detective they'd spoken to earlier. "The other two men involved in this case took my injured man to the hospital. You need to grab them before they disappear."

The detective gave him a hard look. "What are their names?"

Harrison gave him all five who had been involved in the rape case. "The dead man you found in Zoe's brother's bedroom was Paul, the instigator, the leader. His father is a general in the military. That guy here, Jeff, was another one of the five who raped Tamara Vettering. The two men who took my friend to the hospital—Randy and Lee—were the weaker links of the five rapists. Paul blackmailed Randy and

Lee into doing the gang rapes, forcing them to comply. And the last rapist, Lawrence, shot my man, Dakota. Lawrence is a bit of a wild card. I highly doubt he can be taken alive. Not if this scenario is any indication." The detective motioned to Saul and Zoe, standing off to the side.

Saul's arms were crossed over his chest, a hard look on his face.

"Were you all here when the shooting went down?"

Saul gave everyone a simple version of what happened. "This was the address Levi found for Paul. We wanted to talk to his father, find out if he knew anything about his son's activities or who might be involved in the cover-up. But we haven't located the general yet." He shrugged. "As soon as we arrived, the door opened. I didn't recognize Lawrence. I had seen his picture, but he certainly didn't look military any longer. But he must have known he was in trouble as he slammed the door in my face, shooting right through the door. Dakota went down immediately. Two men raced out the rear door and around to the front and helped me move Dakota out of the way. They said the two men inside were crazy and always had been. I promised them I'd speak to the authorities on their behalf if they took Dakota to the hospital and cooperated with us by telling all. They agreed—which I've caught on video on my phone—saying they should have walked away a long time ago. They were scared enough I believed them." He glared at the house. "Those two will talk. They'll give up everything they know to save their hides, and they did help save Dakota. This guy"—Saul pointed at Jeff—"he's angry he didn't get away with Lawrence. Because now he'll be charged."

Jeff glared at him. "I'm not going down alone."

Saul stared at him and gave a clipped nod. "I'm counting

on that."

Jeff dropped his gaze to the ground and shook his head. "Shit."

"You shot at Dakota," Harrison said. "That's attempted murder. As far as I'm concerned, you're also involved in the shooting and murder of a senator and beating up his wife. Quite possibly you're involved in the other three related murders. And you have information on someone else we need."

The cop looked at Harrison and asked, "Who?"

"Zoe's brother, Alex. We haven't found him." As he said that, he felt a small hand slide into his. He glanced to see Zoe standing beside him, her fingers nestled inside his, but she stared straight at the cop. Harrison squeezed her fingers gently. "The only good thing right now is the fact that this is blown wide open. We need to find Alex and the last three members of the rape gang. But Lawrence Hitchcock is hot-headed and wild, and he'll take out as many cops as he can before he goes down."

The cop glanced at Jeff and asked, "Is that what you think?"

Jeff glared and then nodded. "Yeah, he would. He was recently kicked out of the military. He's from a military family, and they aren't happy. His father isn't talking to him, neither is his grandfather. Lawrence is just plain angry."

"Angry about what? That he got caught?"

Jeff nodded. "I got some immunity from the military because of the personal information I have on Paul and his father. Lawrence didn't."

"So he was in there to get back at you?" she cried out. "If Dakota and Saul hadn't come along when they had, chances are he would have killed you."

Jeff glared at her and said, "I'm not so easy to kill."

"No, but I'm guessing the other two are."

He winced. "What can I say? Only weak men buckle to Paul. Although he can be terrifying. Paul wanted an audience. He needed to be the leader of the group. Most people wanted to be close to Paul because of his father. But Paul's true character came out fast. He was very sadistic. Even the girls we did go after, he'd haunt them afterward, sending text messages, saying he wanted to meet up again. Some of the pictures are on the Internet." He shook his head. "I'm not even sure how my life came to this. It's not what I had intended to do."

"Did you know Paul before the military?"

He shook his head. "No. In the beginning I idolized him. I took a bunch of shit from a lot of guys. Typical military hazing. Paul stood up for me, got me out of a couple bad spots. He was always there, looking out for me. It happened so suddenly. Before I knew it, I was in way over my head, and there was no going back, no getting out. People like Paul don't really care about anyone. They are tormented and twisted up inside. Lawrence, well, he really liked it. He was a mini-Paul. He has the capacity to be way worse. And now, if you don't get him first, he'll get you. He is on a rampage, and he doesn't give a shit who he takes out. He's got this list of people he hates."

"Who's first?"

Jeff snorted. "Zoe's at the top."

Harrison stiffened.

She laughed. "Let him come, the little piece of shit. I will take him apart limb by limb."

Jeff nodded. "You know, I almost believe you. But he won't come without firepower. And he never plays a fair game. He cheats at poker and will shoot you in the back."

"Even if I do die," she said, "the cops already know everything. It'll be one more murder added to your legal case."

"Not me. I didn't have anything to do with it. I already told you so. If something happens to you, it has nothing to do with me."

"Unless killing me was something you guys discussed."

His gaze widened, and he shook his head. "Don't … hell, no! No, no, no. I'm not going in that direction."

"Too damn bad. You already did."

Harrison glanced at her, surprised she wasn't afraid. Instead she was smug. As if she knew something.

She smiled and said, "You can discuss all this with the prosecutor when you're charged with the rest of the guys who are responsible."

He shook his head. "No. No, that's not fair."

She laughed. "What's fair about my mother? What the hell's fair about my father?"

"You should be happy about your father," Jeff snapped. "It's one of the reasons you were on Paul's list. He chose Tamara first though. Afterward he said it should have been you."

Then he realized what he'd said.

Her face hardened as she turned way. She glanced at the cops and said, "Enough for you?"

The cop in charge gave a hard nod and assigned two men to escort the prisoner.

"I highly suggest you double the security at the hospital as he heals," Zoe said as Jeff stumbled past her. "Lawrence will try to take him out. Because, like the other two, he's a liability now."

Harrison wrapped an arm around her and drew her

close. "It's all good."

She wrapped her arms around him and hugged him, squeezing as hard as she could. He let her. He knew she needed something to hang on to, dealing with this situation and getting rid of some of that stress. When she finally relaxed and snuggled in close against his heart, he dropped his chin on top of her head and held her tight.

"Sometimes good things do happen to people," he whispered against her ear. "Even to you."

She tilted her head back with a big smile. "Well, there is one good thing in all this. *You*. You're my hero."

He groaned. "Please don't use that term."

She raised an eyebrow. "You don't like it?"

He shook his head. "It's got a not-so-good connotation for me."

She smirked. "In that case, I guess I'll use it a lot."

He glared at her. "I forgot about your mean streak." He tilted her head back, leaned down and kissed her hard.

Instead of outrage, she threw her arms around his neck and returned his kiss.

When he raised his head, he could hardly breathe.

In a low voice she said, "I sure hope you have a hotel room or someplace private to continue this."

His heart slammed against his chest, and he squeezed her tight against his body, feeling his painful erection in his jeans. He tried to catch his breath. They were in public, after all.

Saul glanced at them, and with a smirk, headed to the Jeep, whistling a tune.

Harrison recognized it—the theme song from *The Love Boat*. He wrapped an arm around Zoe and hurried her in the opposite direction to the car.

Once inside she asked, “Where to?”

He gave her an innocent look. “Back to Richard’s. Isn’t that where you want to go?”

She reached a hand over and placed it on his thigh, stroking slowly up to his groin. He sucked in his breath, turned on the engine and pulled into traffic.

She snickered and said, “I’m planning a trip to heaven soon. Do you want to come?”

He hit the gas.

Chapter 14

WHO WAS THIS woman inside her? Zoe didn't recognize the hot, sexy woman suddenly needing this man like she'd never needed a man before. Was it a culmination of all the events up until now that had woken up something she'd submerged since Tamara's death? She hadn't had a serious relationship since then. She'd certainly never had a one-night stand. She hadn't been able to face men. She couldn't look at them with anything other than distrust. The anger had festered. But now it was like something had been unlocked, and the anger had eased, and in its place was this fire, this burning need to cleanse from the inside out. Not with anybody but only with this man who had stood by her side, helping her. He had shaken her plenty, right to the core, repeatedly. Now all she wanted to do was jump his bones.

She eyed his white knuckles as he gripped the steering wheel. And smiled. Because she knew he was with her every step of the way. "How long?" she asked.

"Five minutes," he said in a strangled voice.

She gave a sultry laugh. "Maybe I can wait that long."

He gave her an outraged look. "Well, we're not having sex in the car, that's for sure."

She chuckled. "Hell, no. I'm not into two-second sex acts. I heard you guys are supposed to have staying power. Endurance. The best of the best? Right?" She gently squeezed his rock-hard muscled thigh. When a half groan slipped from his throat, she laughed a boisterous, full-bodied, sensuous laugh. "That's okay. I won't hold you to any kind of test the first time around. It's been a while for me. So fast would be fine."

He glanced at her. "A while?"

She nodded and smiled at him. "Since Tamara."

He nodded in understanding. "She's lucky to have had you as a friend."

She nodded. "Still wasn't enough."

"You couldn't do anything about it." He waited a second and said, "But I'm delighted to know you waited."

She chuckled again. "Yeah. The guy always says that."

"Hey, I haven't been exactly sleeping around either."

"Good," she said. Her fingers went up higher, gently stroking the crease of his jeans.

"If you keep that up, I won't make it to Richard's."

"I trust you," she said with a warm smile. "I know how much you guys are into control."

"Jesus, you're killing me."

"Nah." She gently flexed her fingers again, letting her nails scrape atop the inside of his thigh. "I don't want to kill you right away."

"Glad I can be of service."

At that she laughed out loud. "Well, considering we were both in the service and now are both out of the service, maybe we should be of service to each other."

His voice softened as he said, "I can get behind that."

She shot him a glance. "Behind, in front, or standing?"

He shook his head and whispered, "Jesus."

She patted his leg and slowly withdrew her hand. They approached Richard's gate. He rolled down the window, reached across to push the buttons and waited until the gate unlocked. He drove ahead and parked. "You ready for this?"

She studied the look in his eyes, caught the heat that would sear her bones, gently stroked his cheek and said, "Bring it on."

They both hopped from the vehicle. And, giggling like teenagers, they ran to the front door. Checking that the house was empty, hoping Foster was at his own cottage, they raced upstairs to Harrison's room. At the bedroom, he threw open the door to check it was clear, pulled her inside, slammed the door shut and locked it behind them. She didn't wait for him to turn around. By the time he faced her, she stood before him in her panties and bra.

He opened his arms wide and said, "Damn."

She walked closer, her heart touched to see this big man shaking. She slid her hands underneath his T-shirt, scoping out his hard muscled abs. "You're wearing too much." She slid the T-shirt upward. But he was so big, so tall, she couldn't pull it over his head.

He quickly disposed of his shirt, tossing it to the floor, while her hands were already busy on his jeans. Luckily he didn't have a belt on to slow her down. She undid the button and slid the zipper slowly over the bulge underneath. Her hand testing, measuring. Before the zipper hit the bottom, she slid her hand inside.

He grabbed her hand, pulled it out and said, "Oh, no, you don't. No way. Not yet." He shrugged off his jeans and took his underwear with them. Within seconds he stood before her, almost naked.

Something about him wearing only his socks made her laugh. With her foot, she stroked his calf and said, "I have two pieces of clothing left too. I take one off, and you take one off."

He glanced at his socks and shook his head. "Both now." And he shed his socks.

She slowly retreated toward the bed, reaching behind her and, unclipping her bra, let the straps fall forward.

His gaze locked on her breasts. He swallowed hard, shook his head. "You know, I imagined you like this. I can't even remember how many times since I first met you. And yet it never occurred to me how you could be quite so beautiful."

She slipped her fingers into the elastic top of her panties and slowly shimmied them down until she could kick them free of her ankles. And then she stood before him as naked as he was.

She opened her arms, and he surprised her yet again. He took several steps forward, scooped her into his arms and carried her straight to the bed. He placed her on top of the coverlet, then slowly lowered himself until he was kneeling over her. His gaze was hot, leaving a laser-like path across her tender, sensitized skin. But the look in his eyes was full of wonder.

"So perfect," he whispered.

She let her fingers move across his shoulders and chest. She knew the fever would overtake them very quickly, and there wasn't any time for play. They had both been holding back for so long, this first time would be hard and fast, and she was totally okay with that.

"I'm glad you think so," she whispered. She slid one of her legs out from between his, her foot slowly stroking up the outside of his thigh, feeling the hard muscles of his body. He was in excellent physical condition, the prime of his life. He was just … "So damn perfect."

He chuckled.

"Look at us," she whispered. "It's like a mutual admiration society."

"I can't think of anything better." He lowered his head and took one nipple into his mouth. He didn't touch her anywhere else except to suckle with deep, long pulls.

She arched her back, feeling the dragging sensation deep in her groin. Her belly tightened, and she let out a guttural cry. He slid his hands under her lower back, shifting, and he was suddenly between her legs. Her hips raised, she pressed tight against his erection. While he held her there, he suckled to his heart's content. Shudders rippled up and down her spine as he left the nipple to lick her breast and then back again.

One part of her body was on absolute fire, and the other was so lost and alone. As if he knew, he shifted to the other breast. She dug her fingers into the curls on his head and held him close. She'd forgotten how much she needed this. The sense of togetherness.

She'd had relationships, but nothing that had hit her so hard or fast. No man had touched her soul like this one had. She didn't know what they had here. There'd been no time to consider it. They might have no more time. She didn't know, but, for the moment, she wanted everything she could get from him. She had never expected to find somebody for a long-term relationship. Had never wanted to, not growing up under her parents' version of marriage. She couldn't imagine anything harder or worse for her.

Moving slowly down her body, he kissed, caressed every bit of skin in his path, leaving a wake of fire and destruction. She grabbed his ears to get him closer so she could kiss him. "Kiss me," she whispered. "Like you mean it."

He caught her gaze in his, and, with the gentlest of smiles, he reached up and cupped her cheek. He stroked his mouth across her lips, to her cheek, down to the shell of her ear, back to her mouth and whispered against her lips, "I do mean it. I never expected to find you here. I never expected to find you at all. I walked away from love years ago." He shook his head, his voice coming to a shuddering halt as he was overcome with emotion. "But then this scrappy, feisty woman stood before me, arguing every step of the way. I realized I'd been attracted to the wrong kind of woman for the wrong reasons. What I really wanted was a partner. Somebody who would stand up to me. Somebody who would make love *with* me," and he emphasized his point with his kiss.

She understood. She'd met a lot of women who expected to be taken care of, in bed and out. It wasn't her style. "And I was always afraid men would be the same as my father. So I avoided strong men who I thought were overpowering. Domineering. Especially those men who completely lacked respect for my body, emotions, and spiritual being." She cupped his cheek in the same fashion he'd done with hers earlier and whispered against his lips, "And then I found you."

Slowly, ever-so-slowly, he lowered his head to close the distance and sealed her lips with his own.

She wrapped her arms around him and held him tight. She didn't ever want to let him go. When he raised his head and looked at her, she had trouble understanding the look in his eyes. He seemed so lost. But there was wonder in his gaze. Her eyes moistened, and she realized her tears were flowing.

A frown played at the corner of his lips.

She smiled. "Tears, yes. But of joy."

His eyes brightened, and his lips curled into a sexy smile. "Then let's see if we can't do something with that." He lowered his head again, this time his tongue seeking, searching, finding, and she let him in. She led him into the recesses of her heart. The recesses of her soul. Even as she opened her body and let him into the heart of her.

He slid inside.

Not easily. Not comfortably. It was a feeling of being stretched, being filled to the fullest.

She lay in his arms, unable to move, not wanting this moment to end. And then he moved, the plunge gentle—once, twice. He rose on his arms and stared at her. Their gazes locked—with understanding, wonder and, yes, joy shared between them. He slid both hands down to cup her hips, lifting her up high against him, and plunged faster and faster, deeper and deeper. She tightened her thighs around his hips. "More," she whispered.

He plunged deeper.

"More," she demanded.

He plunged harder.

When she opened her mouth to say it again, he touched the nob at the center of her being, and she exploded in his arms. He shifted her against him, pounding harder and harder and harder, riding her through her climax, driving deeper and deeper as if it was the only way he could possess her at a level she'd never even known existed. Finally, he roared, his body shaking, shuddering above her as his seed spewed forth and filled her.

When he collapsed beside her, she chuckled and said, "See? I didn't kill you."

"Yes." He rolled over, and, with the gentlest of moves, he laid a kiss against her temple. Then he tucked her up close. "Sleep. I'll watch over you, Zoe."

Zoe was so tired. With a smile of satisfaction strumming through her body, and peace in her heart, she closed her eyes and accepted what this man had to offer. Security. Respect. Love. Acceptance.

HARRISON'S PHONE RANG, jolting him from sleep. He checked the time and realized they had both been napping for a solid hour. He reached for his phone and answered it. "Hey. What's up?"

"Dakota's pulled through surgery. He'll be down for a while, but he'll make it."

"That is great news."

"Jeff has gone into surgery for his hand. He's been talking the whole way. The cops have most of it on tape. He nailed Paul and his father, and all the other men in the group. The two men who took Dakota to the hospital turned themselves into the cops."

"Are they still military?"

"Not a one. Although Jeff, Lawrence and Paul lasted for a little while longer than Randy and Lee, Lawrence had eventually been kicked out with a dishonorable discharge. Zoe may not have believed she was doing any good, but the open case was brought about because of her constant complaints, because of her sending emails with new tidbits of everything she found to get them to take another look at it. Honestly, I think the military owes her a huge apology."

Harrison squeezed her, tucking Zoe up closer against his chest. She murmured softly. "That's no surprise. She only wanted justice for a friend." He cleared his throat. "And those other women will need help to recover from this. We should make sure the police—along with a female psychologist—approach them. If any of them are even still alive."

"I hope they are, but I can certainly understand why Tamara felt suicide was the only choice left to her."

"We have to find Lawrence. This isn't over until we get him. And the general."

"The police have asked us to back off the general. And, of course, the military is looking for him."

"He's still not exempt from the law. Any idea where to look for Lawrence?"

"Jeff gave up a bunch of addresses and possibilities to the police. Apparently Lawrence's father had a fishing cabin somewhere close by." Saul's voice deepened as he added, "I'm also wondering if Lawrence will let Jeff live. He made one attempt already."

"If I were him, I'd finish him off at the hospital."

"True enough. I'll keep watch."

"We'll be there in twenty," Harrison said. "Do you want a coffee?"

"Yes, as long as it's not hospital coffee."

Harrison rang off. Zoe murmured against his chest. "I guess we should go?"

"You don't have to. I do though. He's one of my guys, and Levi is counting on me to see how Saul and Dakota do on the job in terms of bringing them into the company full time."

She sat up and pushed her hair back. "Right. You definitely need to go." She pursed her lips for a long moment, then nodded. "I'm coming too."

"You're safe here." He studied her beautiful features, her complete look of sexual satiation.

"I might be. But I'm part of this. I'd like to see it through to the finish."

Chapter 15

SHE WANTED TO see this to the end, and return the favor to the men who'd helped her. This was not over. They still had to deal with Lawrence and her brother. She longed for a hot shower, but this wasn't the right time. They dressed quickly.

"I still don't know how Alex plays into this."

"If he even does."

"Oh, he does. I'd bet big money on the fact he killed Paul."

"But why would he leave the body in his own bedroom?"

"He probably ran. And is now pinning it on me." Hell, she knew that's what he'd do. Anything to get her off his back—and screw her over at the same time.

They were in the vehicle and out of the gates, heading toward the local coffee shop drive-through. There they picked up coffees for the three of them. Soon Harrison parked in a huge back parking lot for the General Hospital employees and visitors.

As he got out, Zoe said, "Quite a different atmosphere here versus Richard's."

"Absolutely. But this is where Dakota is."

She nodded. "I presume they have good doctors here too."

"Definitely. And a lot more experience with gunshot wounds."

She couldn't say much to that. It was the truth. Emergency rooms in any major city in America had a hell of a time dealing with the daily numbers of patients coming through the doors. Gunshot wounds were the normal injury.

Saul saw them coming. He stood in the waiting room, watching for them. "Jeff is still in surgery. There are bone fragments in his hand, and he had some nerve damage." He glanced at Zoe. "He has you to thank for that."

She locked her jaw and nodded. "I didn't kill him though."

He quirked a grin at her and said, "That's a good thing."

It wasn't hard for her to agree. The thought of him being locked up for decades put a smile on her face. She glanced at Harrison and asked, "Do we still have to go to the police station?"

He nodded. "Yes, definitely." He turned to Saul. "And Dakota?"

"He's in intensive care, but the doctors are quite happy with the prognosis. The bullet missed everything vital."

"Kind of a baptism by fire to work for Levi, isn't it?"

Saul said, "We've each been shot before. But it was over in Afghanistan at the time."

Harrison nodded. "You've both done a great job here. Levi's happy with your performances."

"That's good to hear." Saul nodded. "We want to work for Legendary Security. This is what we do."

Zoe studied the two men and realized they were very much the same type. They had an identical look in their eyes, as well as a sense of power, determination, and capability that she liked. She stepped forward and said, "I'd like to say thank you for everything you've done to keep my mother safe and to take these assholes off the street."

Obviously uncomfortable, Saul shoved his hands into his pockets and stepped back. He nodded.

She grinned. "I'd give you a hug, but you don't look like you're the type."

"I might be into one," he said, "but Harrison would kill me. So let's not. Thanks anyway."

That got a laugh from her. She turned to Harrison, who had a quiet smile on his face. His arms were crossed over his chest. "Does everybody see it?"

"Like I said, it's what we do."

She rolled her eyes and glanced around. "I think we should be doing something active, like finding my brother and Lawrence."

"That would be fine, but do you have any idea how or where?"

She turned to Saul. "Did you say a cabin wasn't far from here?"

"It's several hours' drive. I believe the police have sent somebody to check on it."

"What about another location? They can check out the cabin, and we can take the another. Honestly, the police don't have the manpower for all this."

Harrison said, "I'll go outside and call the detective. See what they have planned and if they can use a few extra hands."

He walked up to the front of the building, leaving her staring after him. She glanced at Saul and asked, "You know any of the other addresses?"

He nodded. "A couple smaller houses are here in town, but I don't know that he would go to any place Jeff knows about."

"Right. So even the cabin isn't likely."

Then the doctor walked out of one of the doors where two police stood guard. He stopped to talk to the officers. Saul stepped over. She followed.

"If he's out of surgery, we need to book him."

"You guys are responsible for keeping him safe here. We'll set it up in the hospital administration."

"May I see him?" Zoe asked.

The doctor turned to look at her. "Who are you?"

She winced. "One of the people involved in his capture. Actually the one who shot him."

The doctor's eyebrows instantly rose super high. He studied her, then asked, "I presume it was a viable shooting?"

"Absolutely. It was self-defense, and he'd already shot one of the persons you just did surgery on."

The doctor nodded. "What do you want to see him for?"

"He's turned on his friends who were involved. We're looking for other options as to where one of the men could be hiding out. I don't know if he'll talk to me, but I do know he hates me. So he might spout off something unintentionally."

One of the two cops nodded. "I'll come with you."

With the doctor's permission, she was allowed to see Jeff. He was behind curtains, lying on a hospital bed, his arm heavily bandaged. He was in obvious pain, but the painkillers would kick in soon.

"Jeff?"

His eyes flew open as he tried to sit up and then fell back. "You. I don't want to see you ever again."

"And hopefully you won't," she said calmly. "But we still need to find Lawrence."

He waved a hand. "That's nice. I gave you all I know."

"You gave us three places he could be. But after he tried to kill you, the chances are good he isn't going anywhere he thinks you know about."

He opened his eyes and studied her. "I want him captured. Better yet, I want him dead."

"Why?" she asked bluntly.

"He'll come back. There's no way he won't." He shrugged his uninjured shoulder and stared at the ceiling. "Even if I'm in jail, he'll find a way to kill me. And he did shoot me." He lifted his shirt so she could see the white bandage. "But he missed."

"More reason for you to help us get him."

He rubbed his forehead in deep thought. "Maybe he's with his girlfriend."

"He has one?"

He shrugged. "It's fairly recent. I don't think he realizes I know about her." He turned his gaze to her. "But I heard him talking to her on the phone. And it was definitely sex talk."

"Any idea who she is or where she lives?"

"She has an apartment off Rowland Street. Her name is Sasha." He frowned. "Sasha Leyland, I think."

The cop stepped out, and she stayed with Jeff. "We'll check her out right now. Do you think he'll go to ground?"

"Honestly, where the hell would he go? He'll either leave the country for good, or he'll go out with guns blazing to take out as many of us as he can."

"I vote the latter because it'd give us a chance to shoot to kill."

He gave her a hard look. "You might be surprised. He's a hell of a marksman. He could take you out first."

"It'll be worth it," she snapped.

She turned and walked out, finding Harrison glaring at her behind the curtain. She went to him, a confused look on her face. "What?"

He grabbed her chin and tilted her face up. "No, you're not allowed to take a bullet to make sure this guy goes down. It would *not* be worth it. Some of us don't want to lose you."

She froze for a second when she saw the truth in his gaze and then threw her arms around his neck.

He picked her up, swung her around and held her close.

"Do you mean it?"

"I said it, didn't I?" His voice was gruff, his tone uncomfortable.

She grinned and reached up to pat his cheek. "That's cute. You don't like talking about your feelings either."

He slanted her a gaze. "I don't hear you saying anything."

She grinned. "I wasn't going to until you said something."

He glared at her.

She tilted her chin and glared back. Then she leaned up and whispered against his ear, "I wouldn't want to lose you either."

He wrapped an arm around her shoulder and dragged her toward Saul, while he asked her, "So, what's the deal about the girlfriend?"

"The cops are sending somebody around," she said.

Saul strode up to them and asked, "Do we want to go? Or do we want to stay here and keep an eye on the hospital?"

She piped up, "Or we can get some food and discuss it over a meal?" Both men looked at her, and she shrugged. "I burned a lot of calories today. I could use some food."

They walked out to the parking lot in the sunshine. Saul said, "The cops are dealing with the addresses, getting some people to go to the cabin and other two addresses Jeff gave us."

"I can't shake the feeling it's probably not safe to leave him alone."

"He's not. Two police officers are on duty," Zoe protested.

Agreeing to eat first, they walked around to the main street in front of the hospital. As they crossed, a vehicle drove up slowly beside them. Suddenly the car rammed into her, picking her up and tossing her to the ground as gunfire filled the air. She rolled over to see the car speeding past. Harrison was down on one knee and fired on the tires. He hit the left, and it looked like he may have taken out the right. The vehicle dragged to a stop, squealing like crazy. As the metal rims hit the ground, the driver opened the door, hopped out and ran.

Well, she hadn't been the best sprinter on her team for nothing. Zoe was up and after him in a flash. She cut him off on the far side. He was running, out of breath, already panicked. Good. She had no intention of letting him go free. With her feet pounding the pavement, she raced after her quarry who was desperate to shake her off his trail. He turned and fired. She dodged the bullet easily and picked up speed, faster and faster.

A vehicle drove up beside her, and she knew the guys had grabbed the car to come after her. She also knew it was Lawrence in front of her. He dodged to the left and headed down a back alley, too narrow for the guys to follow them in the car, but she sped after him. She didn't have a weapon and for that she was sorry. Yet pounding him into the ground with her bare hands, well, that would be damn satisfying too. He bolted to the far side. For every ten feet he ran, she gained half a foot on him.

He shouted over his shoulder, "Leave me the fuck alone, Zoe."

And she laughed. She could feel her anger fire through her heart and legs. She yelled, "This is for Tamara, asshole."

It was almost as if she could feel her friend giving her an extra push in her leg muscles.

The end of the alleyway loomed. A vehicle came flying around the corner toward him. When she was afraid he'd jump over a fence to the neighboring alley, she tackled him to the ground, his face eating dirt all the way down as he skidded to a stop. He would have road rash all over his cheek. And she couldn't be happier. She grabbed his wrists, tucked them into his back and held him tight so he couldn't move. And then sat on him.

"The only reason I'm not beating the shit out of you right now," she snapped, breathing hard, "is because I want to see you rot in jail, you little piece of shit."

He shook his head, gasping to get the words out as he struggled to throw her off his back. "I won't. I won't. You don't understand. There are people who will protect me, and there are also some who will kill me."

"We'll figure out who's who."

She looked up, expecting to see Saul and Harrison exit the car. But when the driver got out, she felt all the color wash away from her skin, and horror filled her soul.

Her brother, Alex, walked toward them, a small handgun drawn, black gloves on both his hands. He pointed the gun at her and said, "Hello, sis."

She shook her head. "Please, not you."

He shrugged. "Why not? I've walked this path for a long time. I'm not about to change now."

"Were you at home when Father was shot?" She fumbled with Lawrence's arms, her cell phone falling to the ground. Under cover of getting a better grip on Lawrence's hands, she clicked the Record button on her phone. "Did you actually see Paul's father kill ours?"

He nodded. "Yes, I saw him. And, no, I didn't stop him." He sighed. "Why bother? Johan must have let them in the gate. Within minutes they were arguing about you and that whole Tamara thing. Paul's father wanted you silenced, and things went downhill from there. The general shot Father, and Mom stepped in, screaming at them. Paul turned on her like a vicious animal. Father had beat her bad, but nothing like Paul did. Still she let our father do it, so what was the difference? Then they headed to Angelina and Johan's place afterward. I heard the shots and figured they'd taken them out also." He shrugged again, as if not giving a damn. "I destroyed Father's original security tapes."

"Then why the hell did you kill Paul?"

"Because he came looking for money. He figured, with both my parents dead, I would be loaded. He tried to blackmail me into sharing the windfall."

"Blackmail you for what?" She knew she didn't want to hear the answer to that question, but there really was no other way. She had to.

"I've been playing a little bit of a game on the side." He gave her a lopsided grin. "Father liked to beat his women. Personally, I like to bag and tag them, keep them for a day or two and then kill them."

She stared at him in horror. "Oh, my God! You're talking about kidnapping women, torturing and raping them?"

Her voice rose into a horrible cry.

"Yeah, they're more fun when they're terrified." His eyes went dark. Flat. Empty. "It really brings out the animal in me."

She shook her head, her stomach crawling up the back of her throat. Dear God, how had this happened? He was a monster. "Surely Paul didn't know anything about that?"

"Well, he told me about his victims, and I decided I might like to terrorize one of them all over again." He gave a horrible twisted smile. "You know, she didn't commit suicide."

The blow was visceral. Zoe shook, her body trembling as she understood her brother had killed Tamara. "Did you rape her first?"

He shook his head. "She was already damaged goods. Not much more I could do to her. But I figured, if I killed her, it would cause you more pain. I really liked that aspect." He fired and struck her in the thigh.

She cried out and collapsed onto Lawrence. But she could still sit up a bit and speak. "Why do you hate me so much? I never did anything to you."

"Father respected you. I could never get him to even see me. He ignored me. You, he hated—but he also respected you."

Alex's tone was so bitter she could only stare at him in shock. All those years she'd been standing up to her father, Alex had simply walked away. And she could see how her father might not have appreciated her attitude—definitely hadn't liked her standing up to him. It had made him insanely mad, because she'd never let him see her fear inside.

So, yeah, in a twisted way, he had respected her.

And that had made her brother hate her.

"And I so wanted Father to beg for his life while I held his own gun to his head, but… no matter. I buried all my victims' bodies on his properties. Now that he's dead, he can't defend himself. After I kill you two, I'll go finish off dear Mother. I paid good money to get her permanently out of my life, and somebody stole the goddamn hit money from my Swiss account. Now I could be a target. When I find the greedy asshole who did this to me, I'll kill him too."

Alex stopped long enough to see his sister's worried expression.

"Don't worry. I've got enough evidence planted against the lot of you to keep me in the clear. And to get all the family's money and holdings. Father didn't know how to really enjoy life."

As she lay here—in a blind panic while she listened to her insane brother talk about killing Mom—her body thankfully took over, and the adrenaline flowed through her. She remembered her training, looked for any weapon she could use. She almost cried out loud in relief when she caught sight of Lawrence's gun, half underneath him. She had to stop Alex from killing Mom. And she couldn't very well do that if he killed her now. She slipped her left hand under Lawrence's chest, reaching for the gun, and she whispered, "Stay still."

He lifted his shoulder slightly so she could grab it.

Her brother kept talking, not paying her any attention. "The general killing Father also gave me ammunition for blackmailing Paul to keep him off my back. No way was I sharing my inheritance with him—or you. And I knew all kinds of shit about him and his little gang rapes. Knowledge is power. I can't believe you didn't remember him. I spent a fair bit of time with him growing up. But then you were off in boarding school. He was never as bad as I was. He's a weakling. When he realized what I was doing with my women, he wanted to join me. But he wasn't prepared to kill Tamara. And if he couldn't, then he could never join me. I kill all my victims. Nobody gets a chance to talk.

"So killing Tamara was like my mocking gesture to him, telling him how he was too weak to be with me. When he came to me that night, after he'd beaten up Mom, he was so full of bravado, letting me know exactly what he'd done. But he was still weak. I killed him. I've been practicing with different techniques." He raised the gun point-blank. "Should I shoot Lawrence first or you?"

She heard a vehicle coming toward them, turning into the alleyway. *Harrison.* Always there for her, looking after her. But she couldn't let him get shot, and with him so close, her brother wouldn't waste time.

"Stop," Harrison roared out the car window as the vehicle came to a grinding halt with a bouncing lurch.

Alex grinned and lined up to take his shot.

HARRISON'S HEART STOPPED beating several times over when they drove around the corner to see her brother standing with a gun pointed at her on the ground. As they drove closer, they could see she'd tackled and brought down Lawrence. Only her brother held them both captive. When Alex had fired off that first shot, Harrison knew for sure she would be dead. Instead she took the hit and kept her position. "Holy shit," he whispered.

"Yeah, not too many of us can do that," Saul snapped.

"Stop," Harrison yelled. Anything to get Alex to not make that killing shot.

They brought the vehicle to a halt as she raised her gun and buried a bullet in her brother's brain. Only to collapse on top of Lawrence again. They raced from the vehicle toward her.

Weak and bleeding, she pressed the gun barrel against Lawrence's neck and said, "Don't move, asshole."

"Zoe, dear God," Harrison yelled as he raced to her.

She shifted and partially sat up, favoring one side. "I'm okay. But one of you needs to take care of Lawrence here."

Harrison grabbed the gun from her hand, tossed it toward Saul and swept her into his arms. Harrison saw the blood pumping sluggishly from her leg. He laid her gently down, grabbed his T-shirt, ripped off a piece and tied it around the top of her thigh.

She looked up at him and said, "Sorry. I didn't mean to get shot."

He gave her a startled look. "Sweetheart, nobody means to."

She gave him a sappy smile. "True."

Harrison looked at Saul and asked, "You okay here?"

Saul nodded. He already had Lawrence handcuffed and his feet zip-tied.

"I'll get her to the hospital. The cops should be on their way to take him in." Harrison loaded her into the front passenger seat and took off. As he left the alleyway, he saw the cops arrive.

Damn good thing. He didn't want to leave Saul with no backup.

He glanced at Zoe, leaning against the headrest with her eyes closed. "Hold on. We'll get you some medical attention."

"I'm fine. I'm not asleep. I'm not in shock."

"I doubt that."

"It's my heart that hurts. Alex killed Tamara. I thought she committed suicide. I felt so bad because I couldn't help her." She shook her head, tears filling her eyes and dripping down her cheeks unabated. "Instead my brother killed her. Some sort of twisted proof he was better than Paul—who raped and tormented women but couldn't actually kill his victims." A broken sob escaped. "In some strange way I think my father's death was Paul's payback to my brother." She stared out the window. "What is wrong with those men? How could they be so twisted and evil?" She gave a broken sob. "He killed so many others. I don't even know who or how many. He said they were buried on my father's properties."

"The police will deal with it. As for your brother...well...it's hard to say what makes a man do things like that." Harrison didn't like how the blood still flowed freely from her leg and how quiet she got. Slowly her body rocked with the motion of the vehicle, as if she had fallen limp. "Stay awake," he ordered.

"I'm awake. I promise."

"You have to stay with me."

"I wish you meant that for real," she said on a broken cry. "I don't know what I'll do when you go back to Texas."

He shot a look at her and said, "Come with me."

She rolled her head to the side and stared at him in surprise. "You don't mean that. You only said it because I got shot."

He laughed. "Hell, no. I don't ask everybody who gets shot to come live with me."

She stared at him, the tears still running down her face, and he got even more worried. "Honey, please hold on.

You'll be there soon."

She reached across and put her hand on top of his thigh. Nothing sensual about it this time. Her hand was covered in blood, and her eyelids were closing.

"Zoe, stay awake."

"I'm awake. I'm just thinking."

"About what?"

"About why you would want me to move in with you."

"Because I don't want to lose you. And I want to spend time getting to know you better. Because I think what we have is something we can continue to have forever. Because…" He took a deep breath and added, "I love you."

He glanced over and saw her staring at him—a light of hope and something else he didn't really recognize in her expression. But he thought—maybe, if he was lucky—it was love.

"We're at the hospital," she said.

He pulled into the emergency lane and hit the horn. Hopefully someone had called ahead.

Several people raced toward him. He turned to her and said, "You could give me an answer, you know? Please don't force me to wait. Put me out of my misery right now."

She slid her hand across his cheek and tugged his head toward her. "I will be grumpy and ugly sometimes."

"I will be too," he whispered.

"You will get angry with me sometimes."

He chuckled. "You'll do the same with me."

She stared at him and whispered, "Are you sure?"

He nodded. "I'm very sure."

The car doors were ripped open. Then she whispered, "Yes," and kissed him.

She was unbuckled, and somebody coughed, cleared his

throat.

Harrison pulled back and told the EMT, "Take it easy with her legs. She's been shot. But she killed one of the men we were after and captured another."

The hospital staff looked at her with respect. They helped her get from the vehicle and on a stretcher where she was wheeled into the emergency room.

Harrison leaned against the roof of the car and watched as she headed in to get the treatment she needed.

Three cops milled around. One asked, "How come you guys always get the ladies?"

Harrison glanced at him, quirked a grin and said, "The ladies love a hero."

Chapter 16

"WE COULD HAVE lived anywhere." Zoe shot him a disgruntled look and slid lower in the seat. She still wasn't sure she'd be welcome. But Harrison had been adamant on that point. They entered through the large double gate. "Looks like a military compound."

He laughed. "It's not that bad."

"It's even worse."

Saul was in the back seat. Dakota, still moving damn slow at times, beside him. He said, "Okay, enough already, you two."

Harrison chuckled. "She's been so worried about coming here." Then he pointed out something—just to her.

She frowned as they passed two adult-size swings hung from an A-frame. Beside it was a bike rack, with two adult bikes nestled inside.

Harrison leaned over, gave her a kiss and whispered, "I'll teach you...once your leg is healed."

She quietly sniffled, held back the tears, afraid the two guys behind her would know. Afraid Harrison would. She couldn't look at him yet, so she simply reached out, grabbed his hand and squeezed. Maybe she would be welcome here after all.

Saul broke into her moment without even knowing it. "We're actually pretty excited about this move."

"Good." Zoe smirked, recovering. "So then you're next on the list."

Saul glanced at her and frowned. "What are you talking about? What list?"

"This is the love compound, you know? Everybody here is a hero." When Harrison stopped the vehicle, she opened her door and slowly exited the car, grabbing her crutch. A dozen men and women flew toward them. She froze. "A lot of people here," she whispered under her breath.

A large male, obviously in charge, walked over to Harrison—already at Zoe's side—patted him on the back and turned to Zoe. He smiled, reached out a hand and said, "Welcome, Zoe."

Recognition dawned as she beamed up at him and said, "Thank you, Levi. For everything. And especially for sending Harrison to look after me. It was nice to have my own personal hero."

Harrison snorted.

Levi winced.

Snickers and welcoming smiles came from the women alongside the vehicle. Zoe studied them intently. Ice she recognized from the picture she'd seen on the Internet. A stunningly beautiful woman. And she had a big smile on her face.

"Sorry if that term offends you, but I like it. It fits my world, like Harrison does," she announced as she hobbled closer to Harrison who instinctively opened his arms. She wrapped an arm around his back. She smiled shyly at the women surrounding them. They all grinned at her.

Ice stepped forward and said, "Levi doesn't like the term *hero*. But honestly, all of us have found ours here. So, you're certainly welcome to call Harrison one." As she walked toward Levi, she added, "In fact, the first nickname for our company was Heroes for Hire, but there are more."

Saul laughed at that. "I love that. How fitting."

Another woman stepped forward and said, "Heroes for the Heart."

A third chuckled and said, "I chose Heroes from Heaven."

Ice smiled again and said, "Anna coined Flynn as her Hero for the Homeless."

"Which is perfect, considering she's got the animal shelter and he stepped up to save them all," the third woman added.

Harrison whispered against Zoe's ear, "Actually you're my hero. You saved me from being alone."

She smiled at him, reached up and kissed his cheek, murmuring, "I don't think I've ever heard anything sweeter."

Levi said, "Come on inside. Welcome to your new home."

Moving carefully, her leg still not as good as it should be, she kept pace with the others as they made their way into the massive building. "I think I will love being here," she said. "Particularly because I don't have to go to court in California."

"No guarantee of that," Levi said. "But considering Lawrence and the other two are talking like crazy, the general won't escape either."

She nodded. "I'll wait and see." She stopped at the threshold and turned to look at the mountains and hills in the vast landscape around them. "It's really beautiful."

Harrison held her close and said, "Are you sure you'll be okay here?"

She turned to look at him and whispered, "It'll be heaven." Then she burst into laughter.

The others turned to look at her.

Her laughter eased, and she said with a beaming smile, "I know—you're Harrison the Hero. Just for me."

"Oh, no, you don't," Harrison said. "No labels for me. No way," he snapped, heading off into the kitchen.

But the others had heard already, setting the tone for her arrival at the compound and the rest of her life.

And it was *perfect.*

Epilogue

SAUL LOVED IT here. He'd never been to Texas before living at the compound and found it a unique experience. Not only was he up for it but he had discovered something he craved, although he'd not known he had. A mission again, brotherhood, friends, and family. Only one thing was missing.

He was alone. And so many here had partners.

After seeing Harrison and Zoe hook up in a rough-and-tumble kind of way, their relationship had soon smoothed out, and they were the most attentive, caring, and loving couple he'd ever seen.

And they were a perfect match and complement to the rest of the people populating this compound. A lot more men were coming, joining Levi's company, and most would be single. That was good because it was a little hard for Saul to be alone in a couples' world. And that's what Saul felt like when he was here. It wasn't a choice, but he'd yet to meet anyone he wanted like that. He had to wonder if it would always be that way.

The women teased and joked about him and Dakota many times over.

Oh, well, time would tell. Maybe he'd get lucky after all.

Levi's voice called through the PA system. "Saul, come to the office. I got a *special* mission for you."

Saul's eyebrows rose. What did Levi mean by that? Still Saul couldn't slow his footsteps as he bounded up the stairs. He was always ready for a mission.

Who knew? Maybe this would be *the one.*

This concludes Book 7 of Heroes for Hire: Harrison's Heart.

Book 8 is available.

Saul's Sweetheart: Heroes for Hire, Book 8

Buy this book at your favorite vendor.

Heroes for Hire Series

Levi's Legend: Heroes for Hire, Book 1

Stone's Surrender: Heroes for Hire, Book 2

Merk's Mistake: Heroes for Hire, Book 3

Rhodes's Reward: Heroes for Hire, Book 4

Flynn's Firecracker: Heroes for Hire, Book 5

Logan's Light: Heroes for Hire, Book 6

Harrison's Heart: Heroes for Hire, Book 7

Saul's Sweetheart: Heroes for Hire, Book 8

Dakota's Delight: Heroes for Hire, Book 9

Michael's Mercy: Heroes for Hire, Book 10

Jarrod's Jewel: Heroes for Hire, Book 11

Author's Note

Thanks for reading. By now many of you have read my explanation of how I love to see **Star Ratings.** The only catch is that we as authors have no idea what you think of a book if it's not reviewed. And yes, **every book in a series needs reviews**. All it takes is a little as two words: Fun Story. Yep, that's all. So, if you enjoyed reading, please take a second to let others know you enjoyed.

For those of you who have not read a previous book and have no idea why we authors keep asking you as a reader to take a few minutes to leave even a two word review, here's more explanation of reviews in this crazy business.

Reviews (not just ratings) help authors qualify for advertising opportunities and help other readers make purchasing decisions. Without *triple digit* reviews, an author may miss out on valuable advertising opportunities. And with only "star ratings" the author has little chance of participating in certain promotions. Which means fewer sales offered to my favorite readers!

Another reason to take a minute and leave a review is that often a **few kind words left in a review can make a huge difference to an author and their muse.** Recently new to reviewing fans have left a few words after reading a similar letter and they were tonic to tired muse! LOL Seriously. Star ratings simply do not have the same impact to thank or encourage an author when the writing gets tough.

So please consider taking a moment to write even a handful of words. Writing a review only takes a few minutes of your time. It doesn't have to be a lengthy book report, just a few words expressing what you enjoyed most about the story. Here are a few tips of how to leave a review.

Please continue to rate the books as you read, but take an extra moment and pop over to the review section and leave a few words too!

Most of all – **Thank you** for reading. I look forward to hearing from you.

I love to hear from readers, and you can contact me at my website: www.dalemayer.com or at my Facebook author page. To be informed of new releases and special offers, sign up for my newsletter or follow me on BookBub. And if you are interested in joining Dale Mayer's Fan Club, here is the Facebook sign up page.
facebook.com/groups/402384989872660

Cheers,
Dale Mayer

Your Free Book Awaits!

KILL OR BE KILLED

Part of an elite SEAL team, Mason takes on the dangerous jobs no one else wants to do – or can do. When he's on a mission, he's focused and dedicated. When he's not, he plays as hard as he fights.

Until he meets a woman he can't have but can't forget. Software developer, Tesla lost her brother in combat and has no intention of getting close to someone else in the military. Determined to save other US soldiers from a similar fate, she's created a program that could save lives. But other countries know about the program, and they won't stop until they get it – and get her.

Time is running out… For her… For him… For them…

DOWNLOAD a ***complimentary*** copy of MASON? Just tell me where to send it!

http://dalemayer.com/sealsmason/

Touched by Death

Adult RS/thriller

Get this book at your favorite vendor.

Death had touched anthropologist Jade Hansen in Haiti once before, costing her an unborn child and perhaps her very sanity.

A year later, determined to face her own issues, she returns to Haiti with a mortuary team to recover the bodies of an American family from a mass grave. Visiting his brother after the quake, independent contractor Dane Carter puts his life on hold to help the sleepy town of Jacmel rebuild. But he finds it hard to like his brother's pregnant wife or her family. He wants to go home, until he meets Jade – and realizes what's missing in his own life. When the mortuary team begins work, it's as if malevolence has been released from the earth. Instead of laying her ghosts to rest, Jade finds herself confronting death and terror again.

And the man who unexpectedly awakens her heart – is right in the middle of it all.

By Death Series

Touched by Death – Part 1

Touched by Death – Part 2

Touched by Death – Parts 1&2

Haunted by Death

Chilled by Death

By Death Books 1–3

Vampire in Denial

This is book 1 of the Family Blood Ties Saga

Get this book at your favorite vendor.

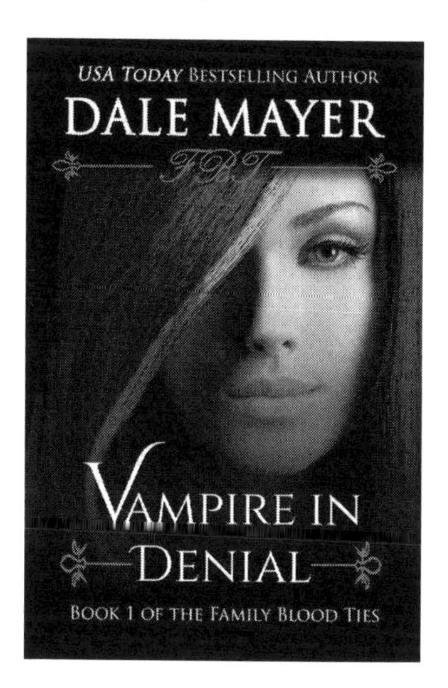

Blood doesn't just make her who she is…it also makes her what she is.

Like being a sixteen-year-old vampire isn't hard enough, Tessa's throwback human genes make her an outcast among her relatives. But try as she might, she can't get a handle on the vampire lifestyle and all the…blood.

Turning her back on the vamp world, she embraces the human teenage lifestyle—high school, peer pressure and finding a boyfriend. Jared manages to stir something in her blood. He's smart and fun and oh, so cute. But Tessa's dream of a having the perfect boyfriend turns into a nightmare when vampires attack the movie theatre and kidnap her date.

Once again, Tessa finds herself torn between the human world and the vampire one. Will blood own out? Can she make peace with who she is as well as what?

Warning: This book ends with a cliffhanger! Book 2 picks up where this book ends.

Family Blood Ties Series

Vampire in Denial

Vampire in Distress

Vampire in Design

Vampire in Deceit

Vampire in Defiance

Vampire in Conflict

Vampire in Chaos

Vampire in Crisis

Vampire in Control

Vampire in Charge

Family Blood Ties Set 1–3

Family Blood Ties Set 1–5

Family Blood Ties Set 4–6

Family Blood Ties Set 7–9

Sian's Solution – A Family Blood Ties Short Story

Broken Protocols

Get this book at your favorite vendor.

Dani's been through a year of hell…

Just as it's getting better, she's tossed forward through time with her orange Persian cat, Charmin Marvin, clutched in her arms. They're dropped into a few centuries into the future. There's nothing she can do to stop it, and it's impossible to go back.

And then it gets worse…

A year of government regulation is easing, and Levi Blackburn is feeling back in control. If he can keep his reckless brother in check, everything will be perfect. But while he's been protecting Milo from the government, Milo's been busy working on a present for him…

The present is Dani, only she comes with a snarky cat

who suddenly starts talking…and doesn't know when to shut up.

In an age where breaking protocols have severe consequences, things go wrong, putting them all in danger…

Charmin Marvin Romantic Comedy Series

Broken Protocols

Broken Protocols 2

Broken Protocols 3

Broken Protocols 3.5

Broken Protocols 1-3

About the Author

Dale Mayer is a USA Today bestselling author best known for her Psychic Visions and Family Blood Ties series. Her contemporary romances are raw and full of passion and emotion (Second Chances, SKIN), her thrillers will keep you guessing (By Death series), and her romantic comedies will keep you giggling (It's a Dog's Life and Charmin Marvin Romantic Comedy series).

She honors the stories that come to her – and some of them are crazy and break all the rules and cross multiple genres!

To go with her fiction, she also writes nonfiction in many different fields with books available on resume writing, companion gardening and the US mortgage system. She has recently published her Career Essentials Series. All her books are available in print and ebook format.

Connect with Dale Mayer Online

Dale's Website – www.dalemayer.com

Twitter – @DaleMayer

Facebook – facebook.com/DaleMayer.author

BookBub – bookbub.com/authors/dale-mayer

Also by Dale Mayer

Published Adult Books:

Psychic Vision Series

Tuesday's Child

Hide'n Go Seek

Maddy's Floor

Garden of Sorrow

Knock, Knock…

Rare Find

Eyes to the Soul

Now You See Her

Shattered

Into the Abyss

Seeds of Malice

Eye of the Falcon

Psychic Visions Books 1–3

Psychic Visions Books 4–6

Psychic Visions Books 7–9

By Death Series

Touched by Death – Part 1

Touched by Death – Part 2

Touched by Death – Parts 1&2

Haunted by Death

Chilled by Death

By Death Books 1–3

Second Chances…at Love Series

Second Chances – Part 1

Second Chances – Part 2

Second Chances – complete book (Parts 1 & 2)

Charmin Marvin Romantic Comedy Series

Broken Protocols

Broken Protocols 2

Broken Protocols 3

Broken Protocols 3.5

Broken Protocols 1-3

Broken and… Mending

Skin

Scars

Scales (of Justice)

Broken but… Mending 1-3

Glory

Genesis

Tori

Celeste

Glory Trilogy

Biker Blues

Biker Blues: Morgan, Part 1

Biker Blues: Morgan, Part 2

Biker Blues: Morgan, Part 3

Biker Baby Blues: Morgan, Part 4

Biker Blues: Morgan, Full Set

Biker Blues: Salvation, Part 1

Biker Blues: Salvation, Part 2

Biker Blues: Salvation, Part 3

Biker Blues: Salvation, Full Set

SEALs of Honor

Mason: SEALs of Honor, Book 1

Hawk: SEALs of Honor, Book 2

Dane: SEALs of Honor, Book 3

Swede: SEALs of Honor, Book 4

Shadow: SEALs of Honor, Book 5

Cooper: SEALs of Honor, Book 6

Markus: SEALs of Honor, Book 7

Evan: SEALs of Honor, Book 8

Mason's Wish: SEALs of Honor, Book 9

Chase: SEALs of Honor, Book 10

Brett: SEALs of Honor, Book 11

Devlin: SEALs of Honor, Book 12

Easton: SEALs of Honor, Book 13

SEALs of Honor, Books 1–3

SEALs of Honor, Books 4–6

SEALs of Honor, Books 7–10

Heroes for Hire

Levi's Legend: Heroes for Hire, Book 1

Stone's Surrender: Heroes for Hire, Book 2

Merk's Mistake: Heroes for Hire, Book 3

Rhodes's Reward: Heroes for Hire, Book 4

Flynn's Firecracker: Heroes for Hire, Book 5

Logan's Light: Heroes for Hire, Book 6

Harrison's Heart: Heroes for Hire, Book 7

Saul's Sweetheart: Heroes for Hire, Book 8

Dakota's Delight: Heroes for Hire, Book 9

Michael's Mercy: Heroes for Hire, Book 10

Jarrod's Jewel: Heroes for Hire, Book 11

Collections

Dare to Be You…

Dare to Love…

Dare to be Strong…

RomanceX3

Standalone Novellas

It's a Dog's Life

Riana's Revenge

Published Young Adult Books:

Family Blood Ties Series

Vampire in Denial

Vampire in Distress

Vampire in Design

Vampire in Deceit

Vampire in Defiance

Vampire in Conflict

Vampire in Chaos

Vampire in Crisis

Vampire in Control

Vampire in Charge

Family Blood Ties Set 1–3

Family Blood Ties Set 1–5

Family Blood Ties Set 4–6

Family Blood Ties Set 7–9

Sian's Solution – A Family Blood Ties Short Story

Design series

Dangerous Designs

Deadly Designs

Darkest Designs

Design Series Trilogy

Standalone

In Cassie's Corner

Gem Stone (a Gemma Stone Mystery)

Time Thieves

Published Non-Fiction Books:

Career Essentials

Career Essentials: The Résumé

Career Essentials: The Cover Letter

Career Essentials: The Interview

Career Essentials: 3 in 1

Made in the USA
Middletown, DE
05 February 2018